ML VK

**In Bryce's protective arms, Hailey felt a stirring that didn't make any sense considering she'd almost been killed just moments ago.**

Still, the intense feeling made her want to snake her arms up around Bryce's neck and stay cradled against him forever.

Frantic for Bryce's safety, she ignored the questions thrown at her to make sure he was okay, trying to take in what had just happened.

To Hailey's relief, with the help of strangers, Bryce was able to hike himself up and onto the shore. The moment he stood on solid ground, his focus immediately returned to her.

Their gazes locked and she realized what a miracle it was they both came out of this unscathed.

Why would someone in a city where she didn't know anyone throw her in the river?

# PATRICIA ROSEMOOR

## DEAL BREAKER

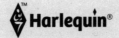

**Harlequin**®

TORONTO NEW YORK LONDON
AMSTERDAM PARIS SYDNEY HAMBURG
STOCKHOLM ATHENS TOKYO MILAN MADRID
PRAGUE WARSAW BUDAPEST AUCKLAND

If you purchased this book without a cover you should be aware that this book is stolen property. It was reported as "unsold and destroyed" to the publisher, and neither the author nor the publisher has received any payment for this "stripped book."

As always thanks to my critique group for pushing me through the tough spots. And special thanks to one member, Sherrill Bodine, who so graciously hosts our writers retreats in the family Williams Bay/Lake Geneva home, inspiration for this story.

ISBN-13: 978-0-373-74613-2

Recycling programs for this product may not exist in your area.

DEAL BREAKER

Copyright © 2011 by Patricia Pinianski

All rights reserved. Except for use in any review, the reproduction or utilization of this work in whole or in part in any form by any electronic, mechanical or other means, now known or hereafter invented, including xerography, photocopying and recording, or in any information storage or retrieval system, is forbidden without the written permission of the publisher, Harlequin Enterprises Limited, 225 Duncan Mill Road, Don Mills, Ontario, Canada M3B 3K9.

This is a work of fiction. Names, characters, places and incidents are either the product of the author's imagination or are used fictitiously, and any resemblance to actual persons, living or dead, business establishments, events or locales is entirely coincidental.

This edition published by arrangement with Harlequin Books S.A.

For questions and comments about the quality of this book please contact us at Customer_eCare@Harlequin.ca.

® and TM are trademarks of the publisher. Trademarks indicated with ® are registered in the United States Patent and Trademark Office, the Canadian Trade Marks Office and in other countries.

www.Harlequin.com

**Printed in U.S.A.**

# ABOUT THE AUTHOR

Patricia Rosemoor has always had a fascination with dangerous love. She loves bringing a mix of thrills and chills and romance to Harlequin Intrigue readers. She's won a Golden Heart from Romance Writers of America and a Reviewers' Choice and Career Achievement Awards from *RT Book Reviews*. She teaches courses on writing popular fiction and suspense-thriller writing in the fiction writing department of Columbia College Chicago. Check out her website, www.PatriciaRosemoor.com. You can contact Patricia either via email at Patricia@PatriciaRosemoor.com, or through the publisher at Patricia Rosemoor, c/o Harlequin Books, 233 Broadway, New York, NY 10279.

## Books by Patricia Rosemoor

# CAST OF CHARACTERS

**Hailey Wright**—Willing to do anything to save her brother—even marry a man she doesn't love—why is the Lake Geneva real estate agent getting such bad vibes from the Widow's Peak estate?

**Bryce McKenna**—Refusing to marry for love after his mother disappeared because of the McKenna curse, the Chicago housing developer proposed marriage strictly as a business deal to appease an investor.

**Alice McKenna**—More than a decade ago, Bryce's mother left the house and disappeared into the rainy night, leaving no trace.

**Danny Wright**—Will his gambling addiction put his sister's life in danger?

**Iceman**—What business does the Chicago loan shark have in Lake Geneva?

**James Croft**—Why is this man with whom Bryce is trying to make a deal so set on buying Widow's Peak?

**Violet Anderson Scott**—What is the spirit of Widow's Peak's late owner trying to tell Hailey?

**Ray Anderson**—He knows selling Widow's Peak will give him and his brother Mike a great deal of money, and he wants to sell.

**Mike Anderson**—Is Ray's brother dragging his feet about selling the property because he has something to hide?

*June 22, 1919*

*Donal McKenna,*

*Ye might have found happiness with another woman, but yer progeny will pay for this betrayal of me. I call on my faerie blood and my powers as a witch to give yers only sorrow in love, for should they act on their feelings, they will put their loved ones in mortal danger.*

*So be it,*
*Sheelin O'Keefe*

# *Prologue*

The dark and stormy night was the perfect cover.

Then lightning lit the sky, and thunder rumbled as his speedboat, engine cut, crested several large waves that pushed it to the shoreline. For a moment, his heart thumped hard against the wall of his chest. Fearing witnesses, he whipped his head around, but tonight the storm assured he was alone on the lake. He aimed the boat carefully and turned into the narrow cove surrounded by trees and bushes that would provide a natural screen. Tying up the boat away from the steps that led down to the water, still concealed by greenery, he ascended the hill in the rain.

The century-old Queen Anne mansion stood more than a hundred feet above the lake, and without using the steps where he might be seen, he accepted the climb as a challenge, especially tonight. The grass was wet and slippery and several times he lost his footing. Once he slid back several yards and thunked into an old maple.

Not that the owner would know.

The owner *never* knew when he was there, *never* suspected what he was up to. She wasn't that old in years, but lately she seemed to be hard of hearing and half-blind—or maybe she was just lost inside her head with grief. Whichever, it gave him every opportunity to take advantage of her unknowing largesse whenever he needed a little extra cash in his pocket. He'd heard about some treasure worth a bloody fortune being hidden in the house, but so far he hadn't found any trace of it. He'd had to satisfy himself with trinkets and old knickknacks that looked like junk to him but that brought in a pretty penny when hocked. The attic was full of such stuff. He would come back time and again until there was nothing left.

Widowed the year before, she lived alone, rarely having company other than the grocery boy who delivered her food once a week or the handyman who came only when absolutely needed, both always during the day.

Only tonight was different.

As he approached the house, he heard a car door slam.

What the hell?

Flattening himself against the building, he inched forward. A woman's heels clacked sharply on the front steps leading to the wrap-around porch, followed by the sound of a bell from inside the house that made him start. Frozen at the corner, icy rainwater trickling down his back, he waited for what seemed like forever before he heard the front door open.

"Can't you read the sign at the gate?" came a raspy voice as lightning cracked in the distance. "No solicitors."

"I'm not a solicitor, Violet. It's Alice… Alice McKenna…and I have something very important to tell you. Something I'm sure you'll want to know."

The woman's excited voice punctuated by more thunder stopped him cold. Why was *she* here and what could she possibly know that was so important?

"All right, then. Come in."

His gut clenched as lightning lit the area once again. How long was this going to take? He wasn't going to wait out here forever in this downpour. Besides, he wanted to know what was going on. He moved back along the building, sloshing through puddles, until he got to the basement window that he'd jury-rigged to appear locked but that would easily open for him. It took him through the old coal bin that hadn't been used in half a century at least. A minute later he shook off the excess water from his clothing and headed up the hidden stairs that servants used to take. The door was cleverly hidden behind paneling and opened into the mud room.

Beckoned by murmuring voices, he eased his way across the room's flagstone floor and through the back hall lined with mahogany paneling until he stood directly outside the front parlor.

"…must be some mistake." Violet's voice trembled.

"I promise you it's not."

Damn! Whatever news the McKenna woman had brought had already been shared. But he listened and he trembled at what they had to say. It couldn't be—that would ruin everything!

"It's knowledge come too late."

"Not too late," Alice said. "Perhaps just in time. Violet, you won't ever have to be alone again."

His gut balled and knotted. Was the Mc-Kenna woman moving in on his territory? That would screw his plans royally. He had a good thing going here and he wasn't about to lose it.

"Maybe I like being alone."

"Or maybe you've simply gotten used to it since Tom died. Think about it, Violet, please."

"Who else knows?"

"I wanted to talk to you first, so no one. Not yet."

"Let's keep it that way for now, until I have time to think on it."

"All right, if that's what you want," Alice said. The old sofa creaked as she rose to leave.

"Don't forget this."

"No, Violet, you keep it."

Keep what? he wondered. He couldn't see anything lest he reveal himself.

"Don't get up," Alice said. "I can see myself out. I just wanted you to know you have family."

He didn't wait to hear the old woman's response. His mind whirling, he was already rushing down the hall, retracing his steps. He had to do something or everything would change, not just for now, but for the future. He had plans.

Plans that the McKenna woman wasn't going to ruin for him!

Somehow, he had to stop her before she told anyone else.

## Chapter One

Hailey Wright hadn't stepped foot on the McKenna Ridge property since she'd been a teenager. She and Grania McKenna had been inseparable until the family had moved to Chicago and rented out the place for nearly a decade. Too bad her old friend wouldn't be here tonight—Hailey would have loved to have seen her again, but apparently Grania had a prior engagement back in Chicago. Even though Hailey recognized a lot of the people who were present because they were residents of three of the Wisconsin Geneva Lake towns—Lake Geneva, Williams Bay and Fontana—and some of them were past clients, she didn't travel in their social circles.

Hailey was here only because Bryce Mc-Kenna had a potential client for her.

"Hailey," a lovely older woman with spiked silver hair and wearing bloodred ruby earrings that set off her red-and-silver designer dress said, "it's so good to see you again. I keep telling everyone I meet if they want the best real estate agent in the area, they should see you."

"Thank you, Mattie."

Mattie Sorenson had once been her boss.

"Nothing to thank me for. You are magic—the best employee I ever had." The woman's expression turned concerned and she lowered her voice. "The McKennas aren't thinking of selling, are they?"

"Not as far as I know."

The potential new client was her main reason for accepting the invitation, but she would work the crowd, see who else she might be able to interest. With the bad economy adding to her worries about and loans to her always-in-trouble brother Danny, not to mention her recent breakup with her faithless boyfriend, Stuart, Hailey had been struggling to stay afloat.

The "magic," as Mattie liked to call it, had abandoned her.

She couldn't give up. She wouldn't. As she walked through the crowd, she plastered a smile to her lips and was grateful to be here. She didn't know Bryce McKenna well enough to call him a friend, but she was thankful he'd thought of her when an acquaintance had needed a real estate agent.

Looking around for Bryce, Hailey took a deep breath. He was nowhere in sight, but of course he was here somewhere.

McKenna Ridge sat on a high bluff overlooking Geneva Lake. It was quite a distance down to the water and the landscaper had cleverly incorporated a walkway that snaked back and forth, with sitting areas at each curve, ending at the dock where two speedboats were moored. The small patios were bursting with people and with waitstaff passing out appetizers and wine. Bordering the house, a large flagstone patio around a wave pool was filled with tables covered with white cloths and decorated with lit candles and flowers. At the far end of the property, the caterers were attending to a buffet, adding platters of meat that came from the adjoining grills.

Because Bryce was nowhere in sight, Hailey was trying to decide whom to approach first when her cell phone rang. She slipped the unit from her pocket and saw that the call came from her brother Danny. A knot immediately formed in her stomach as she rushed toward an isolated patio at the side of the house, the entry protected by a couple of big evergreens and an eight-foot limelight hydrangea.

Once she was certain no one could overhear, she connected. "Danny, I'm at a party—"

"Yeah, sorry to interrupt your good time but this is really, really important."

Closing her eyes, she bit back what she wanted to say, that this party might be the most important event of her professional life. "What is it?"

"I hate to ask you again, but…I need money."

Of course he did. Lately that's all he seemed to need from her.

The sounds of the party—of laughter— receded, leaving her far from the festivities in what felt like a fog of memory. Her father abandoning them when they were kids and their mom remarrying and leaving town with her new husband. Hailey had been barely fifteen and a sophomore in high school. Danny had been nineteen. Mom had made it very clear that her husband would prefer not to have her grown children move with them. A hurt and angry Danny had said he would take care of his sister, and he'd done his level best back then. But the last couple of years, she'd been trying to return the favor.

Her giving Danny money simply wasn't enough, but Hailey was at a loss as to what more she could do for her brother.

"Danny, you need help."

"Why do you think I'm calling you?"

"I mean professional help. A counselor. Gamblers Anonymous."

"C'mon, Hailey, I'm not an addict. And Lady Luck used to be with me. I've just had a hard time trying to get a job lately, so I tried to make money a different way. The economy sucks."

"Lately" for Danny had begun far before the market crash, before businesses started closing or laying off employees. Truthfully her brother had never had a job that he'd held for more than a year. Hailey knew he'd started gambling when she was still in high school, when money had been tight, when he hadn't been able to pay their bills, hadn't been able to afford to buy her a new dress for her prom. Lady Luck had been with him for a while then. He'd gotten cocky, had expected to win, but she'd deserted him long ago. Lately he'd taken his losses to a new level.

"Are you going to help me or not?" he asked. "I'm not going to gamble any more, I promise."

She couldn't stand the note of fear in his voice. Couldn't stand to let him down. Still…

"Danny, that's what you said the last time."

"But this time I mean it. Honest, Hailey, I've learned my lesson. Please…"

She couldn't stand hearing him beg. "How much do you need?"

"It's a lot, Hailey. I'm really, *really* sorry."

The last time it had been twenty-six thousand. Seventeen the time before that. Those "loans" had not only drained her savings but capital from her business. She might be able to get her hands on a few thousand, but that was it.

Her chest tightened. "How much, Danny?"

Silence. Then he said, "A hundred."

"Dollars?" she asked hopefully.

"Thousand."

Stunned, Hailey sank down onto a retaining wall of a nearby flower bed. "Danny, I don't have that kind of money."

"But you can get it, right? I don't know what else to do, sis. I already went to a loan shark. It's him I have to pay back. I don't have anyone else to go to. You have to be able to get it."

"How?"

"What about a business loan?"

She'd already taken a loan and had given him most of the money. "Not possible."

It didn't take him long to counter, "Well... you could put a second mortgage on your house."

She couldn't believe what he was asking her to do. Not that she had a hundred grand in equity on the house anyway. It was still worth less than when she'd bought it when real estate prices were at their peak.

"Danny, I think you'd better come home so we can talk this thing out."

"There's nothing to talk about. Either I get my hands on that money within the week... or..."

"Or what?"

"I'm a dead man."

STROLLING up the walkway, stopping every so often to introduce James Croft to other guests, Bryce McKenna couldn't forget exactly how important the man was to him, the reason he'd given this shindig. McKenna Development needed an influx of money for its next big project—a building conversion in a popular area on the north side of Chicago. Croft had wanted introductions to the movers and shakers in the Lake Geneva area, so Bryce had thrown this party to impress him.

"What do you think?" Bryce asked Croft. "Is Lake Geneva everything you imagined it would be?"

The Chicago elite had been making this area, a comfortable driving distance from the big city, their second home for more than a century. Properties on Geneva Lake itself were rarely simple homes. Far more were mansions, and some were grand estates.

"So far I'm mesmerized," Croft said. His dark eyes deep set in a narrow, angled face, sparkled. "I can see having a second family home here—a place for the kids to have great summer memories. Glad you took me up on my suggestion that you bring me up here for the weekend. So where is that real estate agent you promised me? I'm eager to start looking at properties, tomorrow, if possible."

"What about Leora?" Bryce had invited Croft's wife, but Croft said the kids had too many planned activities this weekend and Leora had to drive them everywhere.

"Leora leaves the big decisions to me."

A statement that didn't surprise Bryce considering how conservative the man was proving to be. Apparently he was also controlling, or he could have found someone else to see to the kids for a couple of days.

Bryce swept his gaze along the upper level near the wave pool where guests were already gathering at the buffet. "I don't see Hailey, but I'm sure she's here somewhere."

"Why don't you see if you can find her?" Croft suggested, swiping a glass of champagne off a waiter's tray and turning to stare straight across the lake at the estates on the other side. "I can amuse myself for a while."

A breeze ruffled his dark hair, cut by a single silver streak at the temple that made him look older than Bryce, although Croft was actually a couple of years younger.

"Fine," Bryce said, clapping Croft's shoulder. "And maybe we can talk business in the morning."

The man was already intent on something in the distance and didn't seem to register what Bryce was saying. But Croft's mind was working. Bryce had the dubious McKenna ability of being able to "hear" what people were thinking when they were off guard.

Croft already had consumed several glasses of champagne.

*Maybe McKenna Development is in trouble because of Bryce's reckless lifestyle. Swinging bachelors don't have the same sense of responsibility that married men do—look at what he spent on this party just to impress me. Now if he had a wife and family, it would be a different matter. He'd have to be responsible and I wouldn't hesitate to sign on the dotted line.*

Someone stopped to talk to Croft and his thoughts faded away. But Bryce got the message loud and clear. Croft didn't trust him because he wasn't a family man. Croft had no idea of how much family meant to Bryce. And he had no idea of why Bryce had never married—Sheelin O'Keefe's prophecy had come true far too many times, including with Bryce's own mother.

Off in search of Hailey, Bryce couldn't help but think that the family company was at risk because of an employee's bad decisions. But this deal could give them the new start they needed to survive. His plan was to combine two Chicago manufacturing buildings in the Lakeview area into a huge condominium complex. Despite the economy, the neighborhood continued to be hot and properties continued to sell. The problem was that, at the moment, McKenna Development couldn't get the kind of loan necessary to implement his plan. Becoming partners on this project with the uber-wealthy, ultraconservative James Croft could keep his company from bankruptcy, Bryce thought.

But how to get past Croft's objection that he needed a wife?

Not at all a welcome thought to a man under a curse. He would never put a woman he loved in jeopardy.

Spotting Mattie Sorenson helping herself to an appetizer from a waiter's tray, he joined her. "Mattie, don't you look gorgeous. Every time I see you, you're more beautiful than before."

The good-humored Mattie laughed. "And you keep getting more charming." She gave him an amused if suspicious expression. "What is it you need, Bryce McKenna?"

"I'm looking for Hailey Wright. I thought you might have seen her."

"She said you had a potential new client for her."

He nodded and turned to indicate Croft who still stood on a lower level, alone once more, staring off into the distance. "My guest and hopefully new business partner, James Croft."

"Well, I hope it works out for her. She's an angel in need of a backer right now."

Something else he and Hailey had in common. They'd both grown up in this area and had a loyalty to it that came from sheer love of the place.

"I hope it works out for both our sakes," Bryce said.

"The last I saw of her, she went in that direction," Mattie said, waving toward the wave pool.

"Thanks. I'll find her."

He took off again. Hailey had been best friends with his younger sister Grania, so growing up, she'd spent a lot of time in this house. One of the places the girls had loved to hide out was in the little patio off the den. There was a passageway directly next to the pool. Bryce made straight for it.

But when he got to the entrance, he hesitated. He heard a ragged sob and was certain it was Hailey. Now what? She sniffed and hiccupped and sounded as if she was trying to get herself under control. And then she started crying again.

Realizing it must be serious, Bryce couldn't stand to let a childhood friend suffer without trying to help. He crossed into Hailey's sanctuary and saw her sitting on a retaining wall, huddled and looking utterly devastated.

"Hey, what can I do to help?"

Hailey jerked and looked up at him, a strand of her long pale blond hair falling over wide blue eyes, the whites red from crying. Her small nose was red, too, and her full lips were trembling. Bryce pulled a handkerchief from his pocket and held it out as he took a seat next to her on the wall, careful not to sit on the skirt of her dress, an elegant pale blue number that molded her curves and flared out from her hips. Seeming reluctant, she nevertheless took the handkerchief from him and dabbed at her eyes and her nose.

"S-sorry," she said. "I—I'll be all right in a minute."

"Why do I doubt that?"

"No, really. I just got some bad news is all."

Reaching out, he turned her face toward his and looked into her worried eyes and pinched expression that told him that whatever it was, it was serious. "Anything I can do?"

For a moment, her expression softened into hopeful. Then she blinked and shook her head. "No, not your problem. I'll work it out somehow."

"Tell me."

"No, really, I should meet your guest."

"Tell me," he said again, his voice firm. "Hailey, I'm not letting you out of here until you do. Right now, you look like you need a friend more than you do an introduction to a stranger."

Swallowing hard, she took a shaky breath, then said, "All right. It's Danny."

"Was he hurt?"

"Not yet."

"What do you mean 'Not yet'?"

"He will be if he doesn't come up with the money to pay a gambling debt. A loan shark is after him this time."

Grania had said something to him about Hailey's brother getting into trouble gambling. His sister, of course, had been worried about her friend. Hailey had felt responsible and had rescued Danny more than once.

"How much?" Bryce asked.

Hailey swallowed hard again. "Too much. A hundred thousand. I can't get that kind of money. The loan shark is threatening to kill him. What am I going to do, Bryce? How can I save him this time?"

Her eyes were welling with tears again. Impulsively Bryce put an arm around her back and let her lean on his shoulder. He really liked Hailey, always had. She was almost like a second sister to him. He hated seeing her like this. So helpless. Knowing how she felt about Danny, he feared she would do something foolish to rescue her brother.

Family loyalty was another thing they had in common.

They had a lot in common, he realized.

Including businesses that were in financial trouble.

"What about the police? Has he called them?"

"No, of course not! And I'm not going to. If Danny isn't killed, he'll go to prison for illegal gambling."

Maybe spending some time behind bars would straighten out her brother, not that he said so. His mind began to race with thoughts that nearly choked him. There was a way out of their troubles for both of them. It was crazy, really...but it just might work. And what would be the harm if they both went into it, eyes wide open?

While he cared about Hailey, he certainly

didn't love her. That would keep her safe from the family curse.

"I have a plan," he said.

"For what?"

Straightening, she turned to look at him. Hopeful again, her expression made him swallow hard. Would she buy it?

"I can get your brother out of trouble," he said, "and you can assure me a deal I want to make with James Croft. Everybody wins."

Her eyebrows furrowed, making her look young and innocent. "I don't understand."

He almost stopped right then, but everything for him counted on that backing by the conservative Croft, who was hesitating hooking up financially because he believed Bryce was a swinging bachelor when in reality, Bryce was too obsessed with work to chase skirt. And it was obvious Hailey didn't have the means to rescue her brother this time— and this time could very well be the last if Danny was hooked up with the wrong people.

"I'm proposing a business venture," he said, glad that he still had some personal resources so he could make the offer that would solve both of their problems. "Strictly business. I'll pay Danny's debt off if you agree."

"To what?"

"To marry me."

## Chapter Two

"Excuse me?" Hailey choked out.

Bryce had loved to torture her when they were kids. Was this his wacky idea of a way to make her smile through her tears?

Staring into his serious green eyes, she blinked and studied his expression. Thick dark hair brushed his broad brow, now furrowed, his wide mouth was set in a straight line, his square jaw clenched, and there wasn't a hint of the dimple that kissed his right cheek when he smiled.

"I'm absolutely serious," he said, sitting next to her on the bench.

The warmth of his leg touching hers sent a tingling sensation along her flesh. Hailey stiffened and adjusted away from him slightly. "C'mon, Bryce, you were never attracted to me," she said, though she'd often wished he was.

"I told you this is business. James Croft, the potential client I invited you to meet? He's stalling on signing a contract with me because he thinks I'm some swinging bachelor and therefore he doesn't trust me."

Dressed in tan pleated linen trousers and a topaz silk T-shirt, forgotten designer sunglasses threaded through his precisely cut dark hair, Bryce McKenna looked every bit the swinging bachelor—one who would make any woman's pulse rush a little faster.

"What kind of deal?" she asked.

"A business deal involving a lot of money… kind of like I'm offering you."

She gaped at him. "You don't marry someone because it's good business."

"Actually, a lot of people do. Always did. Always will." He shrugged. "Considering the family history, it's the only reason I would marry at all."

So he'd bought into the idea of his family being cursed by some woman rejected by his ancestor the century before. Hailey knew the story from Grania, of course, but she hadn't thought Bryce was gullible enough to believe in it.

"Okay, then *I* wouldn't marry any man just because it's good business."

"I'm not just any man. We've known each other since we were kids. You can trust me to do right by you, Hailey. So what about marrying *me*…to save your brother?"

Hailey started. For a moment, she'd forgotten all about Danny. But marrying a man without love involved wasn't the solution. She looked away from him, focused on a large container filled with a spikey native grass, brightly colored flowers and dripping sweet potato vine.

"I'll find another way," she said.

"How? The real estate market up here hasn't bounced back yet. And I understand Danny has already tapped you out."

Heat flushed through Hailey as she realized Grania obviously had filled her brother in on her woes. Not that she'd asked her old friend to keep her confidence when they'd had dinner last month. Grania must really be worried about her. Realizing Bryce was waiting for her response, Hailey turned back toward him and swallowed hard when she recognized pity in his eyes.

"Bryce, I can't be your only solution. You were never without a woman on your arm."

"But never one I cared about."

Not that he was saying he cared about her,

Hailey knew. "Still, I'm sure you have other options."

"Not at the moment, I don't. I haven't seen anyone in…well, not in a while. You're the only one who can save me, Hailey." Bryce reached out and took her hands in his. "And in return, I promise I'll do whatever I must to save Danny from himself."

Hailey was floored by the offer, but what else could she do to get the money Danny needed? She couldn't let her brother die. She stared down at their intertwined hands and felt her pulse kick a little faster.

There was a time years ago when she'd had a tremendous crush on Bryce McKenna. A couple of boys had been giving her a hard time and she'd been about to get into a physical altercation with them when Bryce had come along and had handled the situation, threatening them within an inch of their lives. After that, he'd been her hero. Being that he'd been four years older than she—nineteen to her fifteen—nothing further had ever passed between them.

He'd been away at college, and then when his mother had gone missing the following summer, his father had moved the family to Chicago, all except for his younger brother

Ian, who'd been living with relatives in New Orleans and had never returned except to visit.

Hailey had spent her teenage years dreaming about something happening between her and Bryce.

Just not something like this.

All that had been a dozen years ago, so she said, "It's a tempting offer—"

"Then take it. I promise it'll be strictly business. It'll make Croft happy. While I'm getting this project together, you can act as my hostess. Being with me would put you in contact with people who have the money to buy real estate. A bonus for *you,* not just for your brother."

As Bryce spoke, a chill shot through Hailey. This was all wrong.

"Marriage could be a very convenient strategy for both of us," he continued. "And if it doesn't work and you want out…I promise to let you go without a fight when the time is right."

Danny. She had to think about her brother. Bryce promised to save him. But still, what would she be getting herself into?

"The right time," she said, "when would that be?"

"When I'm certain my business relation-ship with Croft doesn't depend on whether I'm married. After McKenna Development is rolling on the new project. Probably a few months. Six tops. Then I promise we'll play it however you want."

"If you need money, then where would you get the money to pay Danny's gambling debt?"

"Not from the company, that's for certain."

So he would deplete his personal finances, Hailey thought.

She should feel trapped, without options, because that was the truth. She had no other way of saving her brother.

Even so, something inside Hailey—hope?—fluttered enticingly as she said, "Yes, all right. I'll do it for Danny."

WHILE Bryce went in search of James Croft so he could introduce his would-be partner to his new fiancée, Hailey hoped that she wouldn't have reason for regretting her agree-ment and rejoined the party.

Her success in the real estate market really had been magic as Mattie had implied. When she was younger, Hailey used to joke that she could see dead people like that kid in that movie, but in reality she'd only been able to sense spirits that still lingered in this world. She knew when they were happy or sad or afraid.

The ability extended to the properties she'd represented over the years. If a spirit still frequented a place—she never thought of it as being haunted—she sensed if the house was loved or hated and why. That ability had allowed her to match clients to the right property.

Since getting into the real estate business, she'd been able to bring a potential sale to life as no other real estate agent could.

But lately the "magic" had been put on hold.

The spirits had been absent, as if her darkening mood had chased them away. Suddenly sales had eluded her, leaving her in fear of losing her business.

Bryce's plan had lightened her mood—now at least she wouldn't have to worry about Danny—and Hailey could imagine a reversal in fortune. So with a big smile and renewed hope in her heart, she approached a few potential clients, engaged them in conversation for a few minutes and handed out a dozen business cards.

Then, through the crowd, she spied Ray Anderson grazing at the buffet. Hailey's eyebrows shot up, reflecting her surprise. Even though Ray was a longtime Lake Geneva bar owner, he wasn't part of this social set any more than she was. While the majority of attendees were dressed in designer clothes—everything from jeans to summer suits—Ray was in his usual warm weather gear—short shorts, a loud Hawaiian shirt and boating shoes. His short, light brown hair was spiked and he was sporting a five o'clock shadow. Knowing Ray and his brother Mike had just inherited a property on the lake, she figured that might have moved him up in the world here.

She approached the buffet table and picked up a plump grilled prawn. Ray was still filling his plate.

"Hi, Ray." She took a bite and murmured her approval. "The prawns are heavenly."

"Hey, Hailey. I'm more of a beef guy myself."

Indeed, she saw he'd chosen a giant burger stuffed with all the trimmings over the fancier fare.

"I pretty much like everything," she said, "but I don't have prawns often enough."

"Or burgers, at least not at my place any more."

"Not because I don't want to. Business has been a little slow, so I'm trying to learn to cook."

"Yeah, things have been off for everyone," Ray said, moving away from the buffet table. "This season was better than last at least, but now it's slowing down a lot more than usual." He stopped in the middle of the patio and took a big bite of his burger. Juices ran down his chin, but he didn't seem to notice.

"Bad news for all the businesses," Hailey said. All summer, Lake Geneva swarmed with part-timers and tourists. But as always happened when September arrived, the number of tourists quickly dwindled other than on the weekends. She waited a moment, then said, "I understand you and Mike inherited Widow's Peak."

"Yep. Aunt Violet didn't have any other relatives."

Which had made Hailey feel sorry for the poor woman. She knew what it was like making a go of it on her own—Danny spent most of his time in Chicago now. Violet had been up in years and had become something of a recluse after her husband died nearly twenty years before.

"Were you planning to move in?" she asked Ray.

"Into that monstrosity? Not my kind of place. And can you imagine what it would cost to bring it up to twenty-first-century standards?"

Hailey suspected the place was a mess. No doubt a new owner would tear it down and re-build—criminal, as far as she was concerned, the house being a piece of Geneva Lake history—but an estate that size on the shoreline would be worth millions.

She said, "I'm sure renovation would cost you a small fortune."

"One I don't have."

"Then…were you considering selling?" she asked hopefully. Her getting the contract on Widow's Peak could make up for the miserable financial year she'd had. It could save her from going under. She knew Violet had died only less than a month before—not nearly long enough for the people who loved her to mourn her—but she couldn't stop herself. "If so, I would love to represent the property."

"And I would love to sell the old place. With this economy, I could use the money, that's for sure. But Mike isn't ready to let go. He's dragging his feet, wants to go through every one of the twenty-three rooms and every closet and nook and cranny, not to mention the outbuildings, before we put the estate on the market."

"Sentimental, huh?"

"More like he wants to find the treasure."

"Treasure?"

"Legend has it there's some kind of treasure hidden in the house, and until he finds it, Mike refuses to sell."

"What if that's all it is…legend?"

"Yeah, no kidding. He's had half the summer to find it. Well, when he wasn't working."

Hailey knew that Mike Anderson ran a speedboat rental in addition to his water sports and fishing supply store, which would keep him hopping during the busy tourist season.

"Any way you could encourage your brother to hurry things along?" Hailey asked. "Even if the current residents aren't interested in buying, they may have friends in Chicago or Milwaukee looking for a summer home. If you want to sell Widow's Peak before spring, it needs to go on the market as soon as possible, before people close up their lake houses for winter."

"I would be interested in seeing the Widow's Peak estate as soon as possible."

Hailey whipped around to see Bryce accompanied by the man who'd loudly expressed his interest. He was as tall as Bryce but less muscular. His dark hair was cut by a slash of silver and his dark eyes were the most arresting feature in his angular face.

"Hailey, this is my guest, James Croft." Smiling, Bryce looked Croft in the eye and put an arm around Hailey's waist. "Not only is Hailey the best real estate agent in the area, but she's also my fiancée."

"You're getting married?" Croft gave Hailey a closer look.

"Well, hot damn!" Ray said, chomping down on his burger again.

"Why didn't you tell me you were engaged?" Croft asked.

"We just decided to get married recently." Hailey thought fast to cover for Bryce. "It was a spur of the moment thing—we don't even have the rings yet."

"Rings?"

"Engagement and wedding," Bryce said. "We're getting married this week."

Looking from Hailey to Bryce, Ray swallowed his food and said, "Congratulations." He popped Bryce in the shoulder. "Took you long enough to make an honest woman out of Hailey here."

Appearing puzzled, Bryce asked, "Long enough?"

"Everyone knew how bad she had it for you when you two were teenagers."

Hailey felt herself turn all kinds of scarlet. Guests around them were staring at them, seeming surprised. The discomfort increased when Bryce pulled her closer. His smile seemed a little forced.

"Back to Widow's Peak," Croft said. "When can I see it?"

"Nothing has been settled," Ray said. "I'm not sure when we'll put it on the market."

"Surely there's nothing wrong with feeling out the market," Bryce suggested. "You could give Hailey access to look around the property and come up with a plan for the sale, including a potential price point."

"Hmm." Ray took a slug of his beer. "Maybe that would help convince Mike it's time to sell. Let me think about it. I'll get back to you, Hailey."

"Yes, of course," she said.

"I hear you're quite a real estate agent," Croft said. "The reason I was so anxious to meet you."

"It's always nice to be thought well of."

"I've heard you have a special ability…that you can talk to dead people in the houses you take on."

Hailey blinked. Who had been filling Croft with such nonsense? A sense of unease shot through her, but she put it to her weird situation with Bryce.

"My ability isn't quite so defined," she explained. "I can sense whether people who've passed on were happy living in the place and why. I've used that information to my advantage in the past."

"Really? That's all?" Croft didn't seem to believe her. "I would love to see you at work for myself."

Again the creepy feeling. Not that Hailey would let it stop her from making a sale that would keep her business afloat, and Croft seemed like a sure thing. "Then let's hope the Andersons decide to sell soon."

By the end of the evening, when the caterers and all the guests including his new fiancée had left, Bryce was confident that he'd won

Croft over with the announcement of his engagement. The thought of marrying Hailey gave him pause—he wouldn't for anything want her to be the next victim of the prophecy—but he reminded himself that he didn't intend to fall in love with her. She was a warm and charming woman and he'd always gotten along with her, but he would simply view the marriage exactly as he'd described it: as a business deal, nothing more.

He could ill afford to give away a hundred thousand bucks—nearly everything he had—but if he didn't manage to sign on Croft, McKenna Development would go bust, so he had to chance it. A hundred thousand was simply a drop in the bucket as to what he needed to make a go of the new project. Or of any project of substance, the type on which the company's reputation had been built.

Thinking that it was still possible for the business to go bankrupt and for him to wind up broke, he was thinking that Danny Wright had a lot to account for, first and foremost to the sister who'd saved his butt more than once.

Suddenly his thoughts were interrupted when Croft said, "This was quite an event you hosted."

"Glad you enjoyed it."

Even though the sun had set long ago, they were still out on the patio in the dark. The only light came from the stoop in front of the door and from solar lights along the walkways. Bryce was relaxing with a beer. Nursing a Scotch, Croft was once more staring out across the lake.

"So many interesting people, Bryce. You seem to know everyone who is anyone in this area."

"That comes from having a family home here." Bryce wanted to impress upon Croft that he was family-oriented even if he was still single. "My family lived in this house year round until I was in my early twenties."

"What made you move to Chicago?"

Bryce wasn't about to go into the real reason, the horror of Mom disappearing off the face of the earth. One rainy evening, she'd left the house without telling anyone and had never returned.

He said, "That was my father's decision. Dad had a pretty successful renovation business here, but he wanted to start his own development company—bigger projects—and the whole north side of Chicago was being gentrified, so it was ripe for a company like

McKenna Development. Grania and I were already in Chicago for most of the year. I was nearly done with my degree in architecture and Grania was studying interior design, so the company was a perfect fit for the three of us. My brothers Liam and Reilly chose different paths."

As always when he was in the lake house, he couldn't help but wonder what had happened to his mother all those years ago. She'd been considered a missing person, but with no hint of threat or proof of violence, nothing had been done by the authorities. After all, Mom had been an adult. Although leaving one's family and disappearing wasn't something anyone approved of, neither was it a crime.

People disappeared all the time.

Only Dad had known differently. He'd accepted the fact that the McKenna prophecy had finally caught up to him. Even though he'd spent a fortune on private investigators who'd searched for her for nearly a year, he'd believed his wife was dead. Bryce had believed it, too. He'd seen the love between his parents and had seen how Mom's disappearance had emotionally destroyed his father.

From that time on, Bryce knew he would

never allow himself to love any woman. He would never put another person—Hailey—in mortal danger.

As if Croft knew he was thinking of her, he asked, "So is your lovely fiancée going to become part of McKenna Development? Her being a real estate agent seems like a perfect fit for the business."

Bryce hadn't even considered it. "We haven't thought that far ahead, but it might be a possibility for the future."

He wouldn't need a sales agent until the project was well under way, so he would see whether or not the relationship stuck.

"Yes, the future. Bryce, I have to admit I had some reservations about you and the new project. I'm aware of your company's financial problems. But with a good woman at your side, I know you'll work even harder to make a go of it. Responsibility comes with seeing that a man's family is provided for in the best way possible. You'll understand that the day you marry that girl." Looking back across the lake, Croft added, "And it seems to me that Hailey would be quite an asset to the project...with her ability to connect with the past and all."

Surprised that such an astute and practical

businessman was so ready to believe in something he couldn't touch, see, hear, taste or smell, Bryce said, "I know she has strong instincts, but we're talking about converting manufacturing buildings. No one has ever lived in them before, so I doubt any spirits are lingering in the place."

"You never know."

*What will she hear out at Widow's Peak? I wonder. I want to be there when it happens...*

Bryce started at Croft's thoughts that rang out loud and clear to him. So that's what had taken the man's attention for the last several hours. He'd caught Croft staring across the lake several times. What was it about Widow's Peak that had him so interested? The supposed treasure that Mike Anderson had been trying to find for the last several weeks? If so, that was the first whimsy he'd gotten off the man.

As to whether or not Hailey's ability was real or if she simply was working off instinct, Bryce couldn't say. He didn't believe in ghosts. Then again, other people didn't believe in prophecies and curses. He knew *they* could be real. So what was to say that Hailey didn't communicate with the dead?

Whatever got the job done—Croft finally signing the contract to back McKenna Development's new project—was good with him.

## Chapter Three

After sleeping on the idea of marrying Bryce—rather mostly *not* sleeping—Hailey knew what she had to do. She showed up at McKenna Ridge first thing the next morning and marched up to the rear door.

James Croft answered. "Why, Hailey, what a pleasure. I was surprised when you went back to your place last night."

Realizing that he'd expected Bryce's fiancée to spend the night with him, she said, "The cat needed to be fed." She poked her head into the kitchen. "Is Bryce around?"

"Of course. He's in the den checking his email."

"Thanks."

Hoping she remembered its location correctly, she headed to the right of the kitchen and was relieved when she saw Bryce in the room at the end of the hall. His back to her, he sat at a desk, working on his computer. Dressed in navy shorts and a white polo shirt, he shot a fluttery sensation through her, making her throat tighten.

She hesitated a moment, then took a big breath and announced herself as she joined him.

"Good morning."

Obviously startled, Bryce whipped around. "Hailey. You surprised me."

"As you did me." Aware that Croft was mere yards away in the kitchen, that he could break in on them at any second, she glanced over her shoulder to make certain he wasn't there and then, in a low voice, asked, "Can we talk somewhere private?"

"Sure." He grabbed the sunglasses he'd thrown on the desk and slipped them on. "Let's go outside, down to the dock."

The den straddled the small patio where he'd found her the night before. He led the way through it, across the wave pool patio where he placed an arm around her back. No doubt he did so in case Croft looked out the window and saw them. Warmth spread from his touch through her cotton sweater, making her go all soft inside, and the walk that snaked down the pathway to the dock made it more difficult for her to take a deep breath. Or perhaps it was simply the potential consequence of what she was about to say. Not for her, but for Danny.

"Ray called this morning," Bryce told her. "He said he couldn't talk Mike into the idea of preparing Widow's Peak for a sale yet. He said to give it some time."

Disappointed, Hailey muttered, "Great."

"But when I want something, I don't give up so easily. So I called Mike myself, convinced him to let you go over to the estate today and at least look around. I told him it wasn't a commitment, just exploratory."

"That was really nice of you." That Bryce would do something so thoughtful for her lifted her spirits just a little. "Thanks."

"Croft is interested. He seemed focused on the place all last night. Kept staring out to the other side of the lake as if he could see it. I want him to at least think I got him a shot at the property."

Hailey swallowed her disappointment and forced a smile.

Bryce stopped at the land end of the dock and indicated the bench parked beneath an old growth red maple tree. It was a perfect little niche, offering privacy while giving them a view of the lake. Relieved to be free of his touch, Hailey scrambled to the far end of the bench and was relieved that Bryce kept some distance between them when he sat.

"All right, Hailey, what is it?"

She'd thought long and hard most of the night, and in the end, she'd realized she'd agreed to something crazy, something not fair to Bryce, who'd been in protective mode and perhaps had imbibed one beer too many.

Fear for her brother haunting her, she had to force out the words. "I want to let you out of our agreement, Bryce."

"What?"

"I realize it was wrong of me to put my troubles on you."

"You mean Danny's troubles."

She nodded. Unbelievable that she'd done so. "You've always been the type to come to the rescue of someone who needed backup, even when we were kids. I didn't mean to make you responsible for rescuing my brother."

"You didn't. I offered."

"Even so—"

"What else can you do to get the money, Hailey? A hundred thousand isn't chump change."

That was the sticking point, but she couldn't make someone else take on that responsibility. "It's my concern." She would see about getting that second mortgage on her house first thing Monday morning.

"It's a big concern," Bryce said.

"But not yours."

"Maybe I'm being selfish."

"You? But *you're* the one who offered to lend *me* the money."

"Think of my giving you the hundred thousand as my making an investment in my company. I want to close this deal with Croft."

Bryce was dead serious, and Hailey grew a bit uncomfortable. She rose from the bench and moved to the rail at the end of the dock, her gaze focused on a flock of geese landing in the water halfway out. Although it was only fair that Bryce got something in return, she'd never thought of him as being so focused on money. She was certain Danny's gambling debt was a small percentage of what he would make if his business venture went through.

Turning to face him, leaning her back against the rail, she said, "Bryce, you will get the backing you need without having to marry someone you don't love." Though he had said that's the only way he *would* marry, she remembered. "You're a successful developer. That has to be Croft's deciding point."

"Croft is overly conservative. I wasn't exaggerating." Bryce left the bench to stand before her. "Last night he went on about how he hadn't been certain of me, but now that I was settling down, it gave him confidence that I would be responsible if he went in on the project with me."

"You're the most responsible person I know!"

Bryce grinned. "Thanks for the vote of confidence, but trust me, Hailey, I need you right now as much as you need me."

If only he meant that in something other than a business way. Not that she could let that bother her given the circumstances. "Does that mean you won't let me out of the engagement?"

"It means I want to marry you as soon as possible. I don't feel obligated to save Danny's butt, but I know it would hurt you if something happened to him. I respect you and I want the best for you."

"Me, too."

"Then it's settled. Unless—"

"Unless what?"

"You really can't stand the thought of being married to me, even if it's for only a few months."

More like she feared being married to him for that short a time. How could her heart not be involved?

"Well, no," she said, "it's not you—"

"Then it is settled, right?" He held out his hand as if for a shake on it. "Deal?"

The way Bryce was smiling at her made the dimple pop into his cheek. Although she was no longer a teenager, she'd never grown immune to that smile. Her stomach fluttered in response.

"Deal," she said, slipping her hand into his. "With the caveat that you consider it a loan. I'll pay you back every penny."

Unprepared for the tug on her hand, Hailey found herself pulled into Bryce's arms.

"Then let's seal the deal with a kiss."

He took her breath away…literally. With his mouth over hers, she couldn't breathe. Her pulse went wild and her knees went weak. If he wasn't holding her, surely they would give out and she would slip to the ground.

Then he lifted his head and looked down into her eyes. "Sorry. I saw Croft watching us. I figured I'd better make it look real."

A statement that quickly sobered her. No matter that her feelings might get involved, Bryce's only interest was in his business.

BRYCE felt Hailey stiffen before she stepped out of his arms. Frowning at her reaction—surely she didn't think he would force anything more on her—Bryce glanced over his shoulder to see Croft coming down to join them.

"I think he's going to want to go with you."

"Croft? Where?"

Realizing Hailey was a little muddled, Bryce knew it was his fault for kissing her without warning. The color in her cheeks was heightened, a pretty contrast to her yellow sweater and slacks, making her irresistible. Not liking the thought that he might not be able to resist any woman, he took a small step back, gave them both some breathing room.

"Croft will want to go to Widow's Peak," he explained. "The reason I thought to come down here to talk was that afterward, you could use one of our speedboats to get to the estate. That way you'll get a full perspective of the property."

"You can't ask me to take Croft—I'm lucky

you got permission for me to take a look and I need to concentrate on the property itself."

"I'm not asking. I'm simply warning you that he'll expect it." Hearing the other man's footsteps on the blue stone walkway, Bryce moved his face closer to Hailey's and lowered his voice. "James Croft is aggressive about anything he wants. I just want you to know that I've got your back."

Croft came into view, saying, "I thought I saw you two down here. Ready to take out one of the boats?"

"Hailey is about to."

"Perhaps I can come along. I haven't seen the lake view of all these magnificent estates."

"I can take you on the other boat," Bryce said.

"Is there some reason we can't all go together?"

"I'm actually on the clock," Hailey said.

"Showing a property?"

"Looking at one."

"Not Widow's Peak?"

"As a matter of fact, yes."

Just as Bryce had predicted, Croft said, "Then I'd certainly love to come along."

"I was only able to get Mike Anderson to agree to let Hailey go," Bryce said.

"Besides, I need to go through the place alone so I can concentrate." Hailey glanced across the water toward Widow's Peak. "I want to give the Anderson brothers a full evaluation of what work needs to be done to speed up a sale. And of course, I want to give them a preliminary estimate of what we might ask for it. It's business." She turned back to Croft. "I'm sure you understand."

Bryce could see that Croft didn't want to understand. His spine grew ramrod straight and his narrow face appeared pinched. Croft liked orchestrating everyone around him, and apparently his not being able to do so was frustrating him.

Croft was saying, "Maybe if you call Anderson back and tell him you have a potential buyer—"

Bryce cut him off. "I already tried that. He was specific that only Hailey had permission to enter the house." Bryce regretted subjugating Hailey to the man, and he was determined to shield her as much as was possible. "Sorry, old man. Let Hailey get things set with the Andersons first."

Then Hailey chimed in. "Assuming I do

get the listing, I promise you'll be the first to see the place when it goes on market."

Croft's expression showed his continuing disappointment, but he said, "I guess I'll have to be content with that and a ride around the lake in the other craft."

Bryce sighed his relief. Crisis averted.

HAILEY sped the boat across the lake to Widow's Peak. A member of the Lake Geneva volunteer rescue squad that helped boaters or swimmers who got into trouble, she knew the lake like the back of her hand.

As the boat hit a series of wakes created by other crafts that had crossed her path, she rode them out, still berating herself. She should have known better than to think Bryce was kissing her simply because of some primal attraction he couldn't resist. He'd made it very clear that this marriage thing was strictly business—and instigated by the conservatism of his potential partner in a new development.

So why did his kissing her for Croft's benefit sting so much?

Bryce was going to save her brother, and that's all she wanted, right? It was definitely all that mattered. Her schoolgirl crush had been quashed eons ago, and the last thing she wanted was to resurrect it.

She forced away all thoughts of Danny and Bryce as she approached the dock. More than a hundred feet above her, the three-story, Queen Anne–style mansion with a wraparound porch and crow's nest facing the lake dominated the point.

A thrill shot through her.

She'd never before had a chance to list a property with more than a century's worth of history behind it.

After docking and securing the boat, she started up the stairs. Only when she got close enough to see details of the house did she realize the poor shape it was in. The pale yellow paint was peeling in places, the wraparound porch had a broken rail and one of the frosted first-floor windows had been replaced by plywood.

Just as she'd suspected—a recluse, Violet Scott hadn't kept the house in proper repair.

Pulling her digital camera from a pocket, Hailey began taking photographs. These wouldn't be for the sales presentation, simply to remind her of what needed to be done if the Andersons wanted top dollar. Then again, putting money into the old place was chancy. Someone might want to buy it simply to raze the place and build something more modern. The idea went against her grain. The house was part of the area's history and there weren't many of the old places left.

Anxious to get inside, to see if the interior met or bettered the promise of the exterior, Hailey made for the front porch. Bryce had told her Mike said the key would be under a big rock set to the right of the porch off the drive. She found it easily.

As she placed one foot on the first step, however, a chill immediately shot through her, making her hesitate. Concentrating, she tried to define the cause of her sudden edginess. Her pulse was humming and her chest felt tight. For some reason, she didn't want to go inside.

Her sense of the house was oppressive, as if something terrible had happened here. But that was crazy. Violet had been in her seventies. The medical examiner had said she'd died quietly in her sleep in her own bed. Her heart had simply given out.

Unable to shake off her uneasiness, realizing that for good or bad, her "magic" had returned—she needed to concentrate on the positive—Hailey stepped up onto the porch and unlocked the front door.

Sadness nearly overwhelmed her...her heart felt as if it were breaking...while tears gathered in her eyes...

Good heavens, what was wrong?

Perhaps what she sensed was Violet's deep loneliness, Hailey thought. The woman had been a recluse for more than a decade. Someone who'd cut herself off from everything and everyone surely had been depressed. That had to be it.

Still, when Hailey stepped inside, something more bothered her. The negative feeling intensified and she suspected that someone had actually died here. But why was her reaction so intense? She'd been in other homes where lives had been lost. People dying in their own beds certainly wasn't unheard of. But this emotion sweeping through her was somehow darker. It immobilized her. Made her want to turn around and leave the house.

It took some arguing with herself, but in the end, Hailey chose to stay. Someone was going to sell this house, and she needed the sale to revitalize her business, not to mention her personal finances. Bryce was going to save Danny this time, but what about the future? She had to be prepared.

Trying to push the ominous feeling aside,

she made her way through the downstairs, taking photos of everything: several parlors, a dining room large enough to seat at least two dozen people, a music room, a library, a kitchen big enough to be in a restaurant. The details were spectacular. Chandeliers, fireplaces faced with intricate tiles in every room, glass-enclosed cases filled with books in the library. This was no ordinary house. In every way, it harked back to the days when such homes were called cottages but were in reality the summer mansions of the truly wealthy.

The house seemed to be caught in a time warp, the only concession to modern conveniences a heating system that allowed the owner to live here year-round.

Feeling more at ease as she explored, Hailey ascended a spectacular staircase to the second floor with its ten bedrooms, most of which were fully furnished with dusty antiques. In the middle of the hallway parallel to the lake, she noted a door with glass insets. Through the glass, she could see the staircase to the crow's nest.

But as she moved toward the stairs, she came to the doorway of what must have been Violet's room and couldn't pass it up. Two walls of windows—one with a door to the second-floor wraparound porch—had such stunning lake views that Hailey stopped to catch her breath. And the room itself was equally lovely, with a canopy bed and dressers that harked back to Victorian times. A sitting area in a bay held two upholstered chairs and a small table with a framed photograph of Violet and a man who must have been her husband, Tom. Hailey could imagine them sitting here for morning coffee while planning out their day together.

The bath was equally exquisite, with a huge claw-foot tub, intricately tiled walls and floor and windows with transoms of stained glass. A small glass-doored cabinet held lavender-colored linens and the bath products all were scented violet, obviously the late-owner's little indulgence.

Who wouldn't be impressed by this house?

Yes, it needed work, but the potential was there.

"It would be a crime if someone bought this place simply to tear it down and build something new and sterile by comparison," she murmured aloud.

Another sensation flowed through her: warmth that felt as if someone or something had heard her and approved. In addition, the scent of fresh violets teased her nose.

"Violet?" she called out in a soft voice, certain that Violet Scott's spirit must still be in this special room that she'd obviously loved. "Are you here?"

Warmth pushed at her, as if the late owner were trying to make her move. Hailey went with the flow and found herself standing before a beautiful hand-carved antique rosewood desk set before a window.

"Is there something you want me to see?" she asked, suddenly feeling as if her hand was being pulled toward the center drawer.

Hailey opened it, but before she could look inside, she heard a scuffle behind her. She whipped around to see Mike Anderson standing in the doorway, glowering at her. Although he was shorter and wider, he looked like his older brother Ray. He even wore a Hawaiian shirt, but he paired it with chinos rather than shorts. Unfortunately, he didn't seem nearly as friendly.

"What the hell do you think you're doing, pawing through my aunt's personal things?" he asked, his visage dark with anger.

"Sorry." She popped her hand away from the drawer. "I just felt like there was something I should see inside. Something that would give me more insight to the house."

Mike reached around her and slammed it shut so hard that a thick lock of dark hair fell over his tanned forehead. "So it's true. I heard you were a whack job, but considering how people around here like to amuse themselves with gossip, I figured that's all it was. Plus I trusted McKenna not to run a scam on me."

Insulted, she gaped at him. "I am not a whack job. And I'm not running any scam. I run a legitimate business."

Mike stepped into the room, got too close for her comfort.

"Were you or were you not 'talking,'" he said, middle and forefingers to emphasize quotes around talking, "to Aunt Violet before I interrupted you?"

Hailey swallowed hard. "Okay, I was. I felt her presence and—"

"*Felt* her?" Mike repeated. "She's been dead and buried for weeks now!"

Feeling trapped, Hailey was glad when Ray appeared in the doorway.

"Hey, what's going on?"

Mike made a sound deep in his throat that sounded like a growl. "I can't believe you want a looney who talks to dead people to represent this place."

Ray's eyes widened as he zeroed in on her. "You talked to Aunt Violet?"

"More like I felt her presence, that she approved of my finding the place such a treasure."

Ray looked around the room as if expecting to see his aunt. "Is she here now?"

Hailey shrugged. "I don't think so. At least I don't feel her."

"Let's get out of this room," Mike said, pushing Hailey toward the door.

"I haven't finished looking around. I never even got to the third floor."

"You've seen enough."

Indeed she had. Rather she'd experienced enough. She almost told the brothers about the dark sensation she'd gotten on the floor below, but then she figured doing so would kill the deal before it was struck. She followed Mike down to the first floor and stopped in the foyer.

"I just want to say that I have strong feelings about a place and its history. Usually people like my insights."

"Not me," Mike said. "If you ask me, it's downright creepy."

"That's an excuse, Mike," Ray countered, his focus now on his brother. "You just aren't ready to let the place go. I, on the other hand, am."

Fearing they were going to get in an all-out battle, Hailey stepped in. "The question is whether you want me involved with the sale, whenever you decide the right time has come."

"Why not?" Ray gave Mike a look that kept him quiet for the moment. "It wouldn't hurt to get your thoughts on how you would handle the sale. Come up with a price and a plan and we'll talk."

Relieved that she hadn't blown it, Hailey said, "I'll be able to give you my thoughts later in the week."

"Why wait?" Ray asked.

"I'll be in Chicago for a few days. With Bryce."

"He said something about that," Mike muttered. "About you two needing a marriage license and a judge. Kind of a rush getting married so fast after getting engaged, isn't it?"

Hailey hoped her smile looked real when she said, "Not when you're in love."

## Chapter Four

Bryce slipped the plain gold band they'd bought earlier that afternoon next to the engagement ring on Hailey's finger. Rather than a diamond, she'd chosen a sapphire stone the same deep blue as the blouse beneath her white suit jacket and the small bouquet of asters in her other hand.

She was simply stunning.

"I now pronounce you husband and wife," the judge said. "You may kiss the bride."

Bryce took Hailey in his arms and leaned down to brush his mouth over hers. Her lips parted, but she kept her beautiful if confused blue eyes open and locked on him as if she didn't quite trust him. He wanted to tell her everything would be all right now, but James Croft had insisted on being a witness to the rushed wedding, so he simply kissed her— soundly—as much for himself this time as for his potential backer. He couldn't help himself. He knew the marriage was supposed to be business only. That didn't mean he couldn't enjoy himself a little.

He saw her eyes flutter closed, felt her weight sway against him. His pulse picked up and he pulled her tighter so that her breasts crushed against his chest. His flesh responded as any man's would and he deepened the kiss. Her arms snaked up around his neck and a faint sound of pleasure escaped her.

And brought him back to reality.

Pulling his mouth from hers, Bryce tried to tell himself it wasn't Hailey—it was simply that female company had been sorely lacking in his life lately. He gave her a quick wink to assure her it was all a game to impress Croft. Her eyes widened slightly before dropping so that she wasn't looking at him at all.

Bryce started.

She was upset, but why? Because he'd kissed her? Or because he'd made light of the fact?

Aware that the judge was waiting to perform the next ceremony, Bryce shook the man's hand and said, "Thank you," then placed an arm lightly at the small of Hailey's back and rushed her out of the courtroom.

Right behind them, Croft cupped their shoulders and said, "How about I buy the newly married couple the best steak dinner in the city to celebrate?"

"We can't," Hailey said, pulling away to face Croft. She gave Bryce a panicked expression. "We already made plans."

"But I thought we could talk about Widow's Peak. So did you run into any ghosts there?"

Bryce knew that as much as Hailey wanted to make that sale, right now she was simply anxious to take care of Danny's debt. "Sorry, old man," he said, wondering at Croft's obsession with the place possibly being haunted. "We really do have plans."

Croft's smile faded. "Fair enough."

"But we can break bread in the morning." Wanting their relationship to look believable, Bryce pulled Hailey close into his side. Didn't the guy get a newly married couple might want to be *alone*? Of course their alone time wouldn't consist of the usual. "You wanted to get together at ten, right?"

"Yes, ten."

They made plans to meet at a restaurant not far from Bryce's riverfront apartment, shook hands and then went in separate directions.

They'd barely made it outside to the plaza before Hailey whipped out her cell phone.

"I'm going to call Danny, find out where to bring the money."

"Whoa, not so fast. He knows it's coming." She'd spoken to him three times that morning, once on the ride into the city from Lake Geneva, once after they got the marriage license, once an hour before when they were on their way to the courtroom where they'd been married. "I have to get the money first."

"But you went to the bank right after we got our license this morning."

"I made the arrangements, but I didn't want to carry that kind of money with me all day, so I still have to pick up the cash."

"You're sure you're going to be able to get it?"

"Yes, of course." He could feel her anxiety growing. "Things are actually working out faster than I expected."

Normally a couple couldn't get married in Chicago until the day after they got their license, but they'd gotten the license first thing this morning and then he'd tapped a political contact to speed up the process. It was late afternoon, but the bank would be open for another hour.

"We're a day ahead of ourselves," he continued, "so relax already."

"I'll try. I just want to get this over with."

*This* was rife with meaning, only Bryce didn't have the code. He wasn't certain if she simply meant paying off her brother's debt or if her statement included him. Once he made the deal, she had the option to walk. And that would be okay with him, he told himself. He'd never meant to marry anyone in the first place. He'd certainly never meant to pick up any kind of attraction for Hailey. It must have something to do with his feeling sorry for her plight.

As to Danny, what kind of brother caused his sister such heartache?

During those lengthy cell phone conversations, he'd gotten no sense that Danny was sorry or that he wanted to stop his sister from marrying a man just to get the money. And when he'd insisted that they not give the money to her brother but directly to the man he owed—the man who'd threatened him— Hailey had sounded almost apologetic. Why she would trust her brother with that much money, Bryce didn't know, but he certainly had his doubts.

Still, he couldn't help but admire his new

wife for her loyalty to her brother. She would stand by Danny no matter what. If he was interested in a real relationship, one that encompassed a forever bond and romantic love, he'd want a woman who would feel that way about him.

But of course, given the circumstances, that was impossible.

When they got to the bank, the money was ready—ten packets of hundred-dollar bills. He set the packets in his briefcase. Considering how much money it contained, he was surprised when it didn't feel heavier.

Once they were safely out of the bank and in his SUV, doors locked, Bryce said, "Now call your brother."

He noticed Hailey's hand tremble slightly as she held the cell phone.

"Danny, it's me." She took a breath that sounded relieved. "Yes, we have the money." Her forehead tightened. "Why do you want us to meet you in a parking lot?"

At that point, Bryce took the phone from her. "Danny, this is Bryce. What's the address?"

"No address," came Danny's familiar voice. "We'll meet at McKinley Park. The lot is at Pershing and Leavitt. Be there at eight."

"I don't think so." Bryce wasn't giving over control by going to a location in an unfamiliar neighborhood where anything could happen to them. "Try Clark and Lincoln. We'll be in the park. And make it an hour from now."

He wanted to make certain there would be people around and that it would still be light enough so he could see the face of the loan shark who would be taking the money.

"I can't give orders to the Iceman!" Danny protested.

"Then ask him if he really wants the money. Clark and Lincoln in an hour. And I want your friend to give me a receipt."

"Are you crazy?"

Bryce cut him off, and when he handed the cell phone back to Hailey, he realized she was gaping at him.

"What did you do?" she asked in a fear-laced voice.

"I just made sure we would all come out of this alive. Do you have objections to that?"

The color seemed to drain from her face. She shook her head. "No. No, of course not. But what if—"

"No what-ifs."

"You're awfully sure of yourself."

"This Iceman is going to want his money… so he'll be there."

AN hour later, Bryce was proven right. He'd parked on Stockton Drive in Lincoln Park, which swept along the lakefront along most of the north side. He'd left the case of money in the trunk. Even though the park was safe, there was no sense in taking chances with that kind of loot.

They'd barely taken a bench sheltered in back by bushes and overhead by a huge maple than two men approached on foot from busy Clark Street. Dressed in designer trousers and a shirt the same blue as his eyes—the same blue as Hailey's wedding blouse—Danny Wright was still the handsome blond heartbreaker he'd always been. In contrast, a design was shaved into his companion's short hair and the man wore slouch jeans and a bright white muscle T-shirt that showed off his bulked coffee-colored arms decorated with tattoos.

When the men approached the bench, Hailey shot to her feet. "Danny!" She launched herself at her brother and threw her arms around his neck.

"Sis." Danny hugged her, but his gaze zeroed in on Bryce, who was getting to his feet. Then he looked around on the bench and on the ground and then back to Bryce. "Where's the money?"

There was a look of desperation in his eyes that Bryce had never seen before. The man truly feared for his life.

Bryce turned to the loan shark and asked, "Where's the receipt?"

Scowling, the man said, "You're whack."

"I'm careful."

"I don't got no receipt, but I got this." Remaining calm and cool like his nickname, Iceman pulled up the front of his T-shirt to show Bryce the gun in his waistband.

"No, you can't shoot anyone." Hailey's plea sounded strangled. Her face had drained of color. "We have the money!"

"You won't need that." Bryce shrugged and remained calm himself. "No need for threats. I just want to make sure there's proof that Danny's debt is paid. I find it hard to believe you don't have an IOU."

Bryce didn't think Iceman was going to answer. His dark eyes narrowed into slits.

Bryce could tell the other man was sizing him up.

Finally, he said, "I got his paper."

"Then sign it over to me." Bryce pulled out a pen and offered it to Iceman who simply stared at it. "Sign it over or no money."

Iceman swiped the pen from his hand and from his jeans pocket, pulled out a folded piece of paper. Spreading it out on the bench he paused with his pen over the paper. "Name?"

"Bryce McKenna." He spelled it out so the man would get it right.

Color was flooding Hailey's cheeks again and to Bryce's alarm, she pulled her cell phone out of her pocket and aimed it at the loan shark. She was taking his photo. Bryce stepped in front of Iceman so he couldn't see her.

After signing, Iceman held the paper out of Bryce's reach. "Money first."

Bryce led the way to his car, a hundred yards away. Opening the trunk, all too aware of Hailey taking more photos, he lifted out the case and purposely directed Iceman's attention away from her. The exchange made, he expected Iceman to disappear, but the man stood there, expression thoughtful.

"That's a lot of benjamins to give away. I can give you a chance to win it all back. Tonight."

"I don't gamble."

Iceman looked to Danny, threw back his head and laughed. "What you think you just did by buying his IOU? You change your mind, Danny knows where to find me."

"You leave my brother be!" Hailey said.

Iceman smirked. "And what if I don't?"

"I'll have you arrested. With proof."

She held up her cell phone and jiggled it. Iceman's smirk disappeared.

Bryce grabbed Hailey's arm and pushed the phone out of sight, and when she looked at him, he gave her a warning glare. He could see that she was all wound up and wanted to say more, but in the end, she let a breath whisper through her lips and clammed up.

"You oughta watch who you threaten, baby, or things might not go so good for either you or your brother."

With that, the loan shark sauntered away, swinging the case as if it were a picnic basket rather than filled with money.

Finally Danny said, "Thanks, sis."

*I'm probably gonna have to cool it for a*

*while. Let things settle down before I get into another game.*

"Don't thank me." Hailey turned to Bryce, her expression one of gratitude.

"Oh yeah, thanks, Bryce." Danny held out his hand, but not for a shake. "I'll take the IOU."

*Next time I'll be more careful. Win a little at a time. Iceman won't even realize what's happening until I get a hundred grand from him.*

Hearing Danny's thoughts, Bryce fumed inside. Would the miscreant never learn from his mistakes? He folded up the IOU and stuffed it into a pocket. "Did you think I was just going to pay your debt and give you a pass?" Bryce asked. "You owe *me* the money now, Danny, and I expect you to pay back every penny."

"Hailey!"

"Don't look to your sister for help." Bryce's hands balled into fists so he wouldn't touch the idiot because he might lose control. "For once look to yourself. You have a clean slate, a chance to start over, and if you're smart, that's just what you'll do because that's the last money you'll get from us."

"But I need something now," Danny told

Hailey in a querulous voice. "You know, just to tide me over. Until I get a job."

She started to open her bag as if she was going to give him whatever he wanted. Bryce took hold of her hand and shook his head.

"You can have a job, Danny, working for my building development company as soon as I get this new project in line."

"I don't know anything about that kind of work."

"Then you'll learn. I have a big project coming up. I can use a gofer."

"A what?"

"Someone who goes for things. Runs errands."

"You call that a job?"

"It's a start. And part of your pay will be held back toward your debt."

"You're not really going to let him do this to me, are you?" Danny asked Hailey.

"We'll talk about it later," she said, her voice now tight.

"There's nothing to talk about." Bryce handed Danny his card. "I'll be in touch when there's work. If you don't like the idea of working for me, then find yourself a job now. Stop relying on your sister to haul your butt out of the flames."

Hailey tried to hug Danny again, but he backed off, gave them both a wounded expression before turning away.

"Danny!"

"Let him go. He needs time to think things over."

"So do I!"

HAILEY stewed in silence all the way back to Bryce's apartment, where she took refuge in the guest bathroom and changed into casual clothes and running shoes. The highrise fronted the Chicago River. Bryce's corner two-bedroom apartment had stunning views both of the river and of Lake Michigan.

She thought the modern apartment an odd choice for a man who developed conversion condominiums. Then again, his father had started the business. Undoubtedly it was lucrative and this condo in the sky was more indicative of Bryce's true taste. A downtown apartment of this size cost a pretty penny, certainly more than she'd ever considered spending. Briefly wondering what grand old building had been razed to be replaced by this one, she didn't know why she was trying to figure the man out. He'd done her a favor only because it was in his own best interest.

He wasn't really concerned with her or with her brother.

Securing her hair in a ponytail, she left the bathroom. Still dressed in his perfectly tailored gray wedding suit, Bryce stood staring out the floor-to-ceiling windows in the living area where the leather-and-chrome furniture was as modern as the building. Had Grania designed the place to suit her brother's personality? There was nothing soft about the room, nothing to make it feel like a home.

She knew what a home felt like—Danny had made sure of that.

Her emotions picking up steam, she said, "Danny is my brother, Bryce, not yours."

He turned to face her and she steeled herself. He was too damned good-looking for her comfort. Too tempting. She had to harden herself against the lure of those green eyes, against the promise of the crease in his cheek when he smiled.

He wasn't smiling now, though, as he swept his gaze from her running shoes to her capris and from her T-shirt to her ponytail. "I'm aware of your relationship with Danny, Hailey. What's your point?"

His cool tone stiffened her spine. "It's not

up to you to tell him whether I'll help him again."

"When did you become his banker? Or his mother?"

Feeling as if he'd just hit her below the belt, Hailey gaped at him. Surely he must remember that their mother had chosen a man over her children.

"That's not fair. When our mother left me with my brother because it was more convenient for her, Danny did what he had to so that he could take care of me. He's all I have."

"You have me now," Bryce reminded her.

"True, as a friend."

"That doesn't make me any less of a friend." Bryce sat in one of his leather chairs. "And as a friend, I have to tell you, no matter how great Danny was in the past, he's gone off the straight and narrow. Until he chooses to clean up his act, he's not to be trusted."

"He said he was going to stop gambling." She had to believe that.

"I heard him thinking about holding off gambling for a while, until he could figure out how to win the hundred thousand back from Iceman."

That stopped her short. "What do you mean you heard him think that?"

"C'mon, Hailey, you and Grania were best friends for years. I'm sure you got an inkling that everyone in our family is a little psychic."

Grania had said as much, but Hailey had thought it was a kid's flight of fancy.

"You're saying you can hear what people think?"

"Not always, but I have my moments. It's kind of like radar. If the person is relaxed and his or her mind is open, I gravitate there. Addicts promise a lot of things the person they're conning wants to hear. Danny needs professional help, the kind you can't give him."

Even though she'd told Danny the same thing herself, she hated hearing it come from someone else. "You may be right, Bryce, but I'm never going to abandon him."

"I'm not suggesting you should. What I am suggesting is that you stop helping Danny stay in the life he's chosen for himself. You need to start practicing tough love and stop enabling him."

Bryce didn't know Danny, didn't know the years of freedom he'd sacrificed for her. He hadn't always been the way he was now—he'd been responsible once. She'd needed him then and he needed her now.

"I would do anything for my brother!"

"Apparently you're even willing to get yourself killed. Taking those photos of Iceman was bad enough, but then waving your cell phone under his nose like a red flag was you asking for trouble."

Her spirits deflating again, Hailey grabbed the extra set of keys he'd given her and stuffed them into her pocket along with her phone. "I'm going to get some fresh air."

"Hailey, wait a minute and I'll come with you."

But she was already out the door. She punched the call button for the elevator. The doors opened immediately, and she stepped in. As the doors whooshed closed, she thought she heard Bryce's voice, but she was in no mood to continue this conversation. The elevator quickly brought her to the lobby. She rushed to the exit, but the doorman beat her to it and quickly swung open the door.

"Mrs. McKenna."

"The name's Ms. Wright," she informed him before jogging off.

The sun had already set, the street and building lights gleamed against the deepening gloom, and the air felt much cooler than she'd expected. A run along the river was exactly what she needed in many respects. It was a way to cool down her anger, a way for her to think more clearly.

As she approached the corner, she noted a dark car sat at the curb, its engine running. The driver didn't seem ready to move the vehicle, so she passed it and crossed the street. Needing to warm up before she went all-out, she started slowly at first, but when she thought she heard her name chase her—Bryce was following her!—she ran full-speed.

Her morning run used to be a ritual, but the downturn in her life had stolen her motivation, so she quickly found herself short of breath. A quick glance behind her assured Hailey that Bryce wasn't nearby, so she slowed down.

And then realized she was being followed...by what looked like the black car that had been sitting outside her building.

Her stomach knotted. Surely she was imagining things. Veering away from the car, she felt her pulse jump when it followed into an area along the river that had a lot of parked cars.

Dark.

Deserted.

Scary.

Whipping around in a circle, she looked for

people—witnesses. A few strolled down the sidewalk on the other side of the street, away from the river. She bolted toward them.

"Hey, wait a minute!" she shouted and a couple of women turned toward her.

"What's going on?" one of them yelled back.

"I think this guy's after me!"

The car cut Hailey off, and before she could regroup, a man dressed in black exited and came at her. She backed up and tried to get her bearings. A ski mask kept her from identifying him as he lunged for her. She shot off around the other side of the car, but she was cut off, grabbed and dragged screaming straight toward the river. He was big and strong and no matter that she fought, she couldn't free herself. Her pulse raced and her breath shortened and she feared what came next.

"Hey, stop that!" one of the women ordered from too far away to do anything about it.

"Someone help her!" another yelled.

"Let go!" Hailey clawed at the mask.

He ducked, then struck out, catching her on the side of her face with the back of his hand. Shocked, she stopped fighting for a moment, just long enough for him to lift her and heave her over the guardrail.

Hailey's stomach dropped faster than her body. As she sped to the water probably thirty feet below, she fought to control her flailing arms and legs, knowing that if she didn't go in right, she would surely drown.

## Chapter Five

Out chasing Hailey, Bryce heard screams and the shouts of several people. On instinct, he ran toward the river's edge where he was almost run over by a black car whose tires squealed as it took the corner on two wheels.

*Help...need help...*

His attention whipped back to what was going on at the river. "Hailey?" Had he really heard her? He elbowed through the people gathering at the embankment and looked down into the water straight below. It rippled with the current and a passing boat, but he saw no other splash.

"What happened?" he asked the frantic-seeming woman standing at the railing next to him.

"Someone threw a woman over the guard-rail. I called 9-1-1. But now we can't see her."

Because she wasn't struggling, Bryce thought. Because she was unconscious?

A scream tore at his gut. "Where did that come from?" he asked the woman even as he looked hard at the water.

"What?"

"Didn't you hear that scream?"

"I didn't hear anything. I think she drowned."

Just then, the surface broke with a splash and everyone at the rail gasped.

"There she is!" a guy said. "And there's a boat coming toward her. Hope the driver sees her!"

Zeroing in on Hailey—though it was near dark, Bryce recognized her pale hair—he told himself not to panic. The current had already taken her away from the railing and into danger. He could get to her in time! He scrambled up on the rail even as he heard the siren of a cop car coming at them. He would get to her before that boat did.

As he prepared to leap into the water, someone shouted, "No, stop! Help is here."

But he went ahead anyway. Feet first.

The jump was major and so was the landing. Managing to stay upright, arms wrapped around his upper body, holding his suit jacket close, Bryce cut through the water feet first, holding his breath as he plunged downward. When the momentum slowed, he fought his way back to the surface and whipped the water out of his face so he could see.

Several yards away, Hailey struggled for control. And from the east, that boat was coming straight at her. Fast. Bryce told himself not to panic, that she would be all right.

"Hang on, Hailey!" he yelled. "There's a boat. Get out of the way!"

*Trying!* she responded, and he knew she didn't say the word out loud. How was that possible when he normally heard another's thoughts when that person was relaxed, not in a panic?

It took the longest minute of his life to get to her. The boat was bearing down on them, but somehow he forced her toward shore, and when the boat passed and the wake swamped them, he held on to her as if he would never let her go.

They bobbed in the wake as it died out. Hailey was coughing up water, her body tense, her arms thrashing.

"Stop fighting the river!" he ordered, fearing that she would drown herself. "Relax and move with it. Let me guide you to shore."

That was always the questionable part of a rescue. A panicked person fearing drowning might grab on to the rescuer, might climb on him to help herself. But, as if Hailey knew he would save her if she just let him do what he needed to do, she gave over and relaxed as he'd demanded. Heaving a gasp of relief, Bryce wrapped an arm across her full breasts and towed her to shore.

IN Bryce's protective arms, Hailey felt a stirring that didn't make any sense considering she'd almost been killed just moments ago. Still, the intense feeling made her want to snake her arms up around Bryce's neck and stay cradled against him forever.

Then they got to the cement wall lining this part of the river. Above, people crowded the bank. A few reached down for her and Bryce let go of his hold, placed hands around her waist and lifted. A couple of the guys on shore grabbed her arms and pulled her up out of the water.

Frantic for Bryce's safety, she ignored the questions thrown at her to make sure he was okay. Wrapping her arms around her middle to warm herself, Hailey tried to take in what had just happened. She watched a bystander get down on his stomach to reach for Bryce, who grabbed his hand. Then another man got down and took his other hand.

To Hailey's relief, with the help of strangers, Bryce was able to hike himself up and onto the shore. The moment he stood on solid ground, his focus immediately returned to her. Their gazes locked and she realized what a miracle it was they both came out of this unscathed.

Even so, she shivered and cold whipped through her…they both could have drowned or been run over by that boat.

"Thanks, all of you," she said to their rescuers.

"Hey, no problem," one of the men said. "Just glad you're okay."

"You *are* okay, right?" Bryce asked, moving closer. "You're not hurt?"

Realizing he'd jumped into the river wearing his designer suit—ruined, she thought—Hailey said, "Just cold."

And confused. Why would someone in a city where she didn't know anyone throw her in the river? And why hadn't she been able to get herself back to shore? Feeling a little out of it, she remembered being hit. And then hitting the water. The rest came to her in pieces, as if she'd dreamed it.

Bryce wrapped his arms around her, then held her head back and looked deep into her eyes. Hailey's breath caught in her throat and a warmth spread through her. For a moment, she thought Bryce might kiss her. But then the moment passed and he relaxed and she realized he'd simply been checking to make sure she was all right.

Swallowing hard, she told herself she was not disappointed.

"Thanks for the save," she said, knowing it wasn't enough. How did she properly thank Bryce for saving her life? "You put yourself on the line for me."

Before Bryce could say anything, an ambulance pulled off the street, and a woman waved the official vehicle in their direction. "Over there!"

A squad car followed and a uniformed officer jumped out at the same time as did the paramedic who immediately brought Hailey to the ambulance to take her vitals. Her blood pressure was up a little, her temperature down. Wet and cold, she was shivering harder now, but she didn't complain. Thanks to Bryce, she was okay.

"What happened?" the officer asked.

"Someone threw my wife in the river. I'm Bryce McKenna and this is Hailey. Would you call my brother, Detective Reilly McKenna, and ask him if he's free to meet me here?"

Nodding, the cop moved away and did as Bryce asked while the young paramedic named Hank shone a light in her eyes.

After inspecting them carefully, Hank said, "Doesn't look like you have a concussion, so that's good." He unfolded a blanket and draped it around her shoulders. "I'll get you an instant heat pack." Climbing inside the ambulance, he reached into a drawer, pulled out a pack and popped it. "That'll help."

"Thanks." She gladly took the pack and placed it against her middle. As warmth quickly spread through her, she turned back to the officer who was waiting to talk to her.

"So how did this all happen?" he asked.

She shrugged. "Some guy followed me in a car, got out, grabbed me, then threw me in the river."

"Did you recognize him?"

"No. Maybe it was a case of mistaken identity…he thought I was someone else."

"Description?"

"His face was covered with a ski mask." Hailey's stomach knotted at the memory, and as if he could sense it, Bryce moved closer, placed a wet arm across her back. Unable to help herself, she leaned into him. "He was taller than me and a lot stronger. That's all I remember."

"What about the make of the car?"

She shook her head. "Sorry. I'm not good at cars. It was black, a newer model. It looked expensive. I saw it sitting on the side street next to Bryce's building."

"Did he take anything?"

"I didn't have anything on me but my cell phone and the apartment keys." She checked her pocket. "Still there." Looking at Bryce, she said, "I can't believe you had to jump in for me. I've been a member of the lake rescue team at home since high school."

She'd helped save several lives in the last dozen years, but she hadn't been able to save her own.

"You may have hit the water wrong," the paramedic said. "That's a pretty steep drop."

She nodded. "I remember not being able to fight the current."

Just then a siren split the night and a dark car pulled up to the ambulance. Even though she hadn't seen the man who got out since high school, Hailey recognized him. Tall and dark-haired like the other McKenna men, Reilly had been only two years ahead of her and Grania.

"What's going on, Bryce?" he asked, muddy violet eyes looking from his brother to her. "Hailey Wright?"

"She's Hailey McKenna now," Bryce said.

Reilly couldn't have looked more surprised. "What the hell is going on?"

WHILE the uniformed officer canvassed the bystanders for information about the attacker, Bryce quickly updated Reilly on the past few days and watched his younger brother's face freeze in anger.

"What were you thinking, Bryce? A death threat on Danny Wright and you decided you could handle it alone? You could have been killed, either one of you," he said, now turning his glare on Hailey. "Why didn't you come to me in the first place? I could have arrested this Iceman and—"

"With what?" Bryce argued. "Despite the photos Hailey took of the exchange with her cell phone, there wasn't actual proof of anything illegal."

Hailey fished in her pocket and pulled out her cell and flipped it open. Water streamed out. "So much for those photos."

"Even if we had real proof," Bryce said, "Danny wouldn't have testified. Or if he had, his word wouldn't have meant much."

Expecting Hailey to come to her brother's defense yet again, Bryce quickly glanced at her, but if she had something to say, she held it back this time.

"You may be right," Reilly said, "but we're only guessing." He took out a small notebook and pen. "Let's start from the beginning."

He took notes as Hailey repeated her story.

"Hmm, this Iceman seems to be a likely suspect," Reilly suggested.

"Why would he attack me when he got his money?"

"Maybe because you threatened him," Bryce reminded her, "and then you waved your cell phone in his face."

"Besides," Reilly said, "you're involved in two criminal situations in one day. I don't believe in coincidence."

"Truthfully, I didn't see who it was," Hailey said. "It could have been anyone. Just a random mugging."

"So the attacker took your purse?"

"No, I wasn't carrying one, but he might have thought I had a wallet on me."

"You're reaching. It sounds personal to me," Reilly said. "Have you had any problems with anyone *else* lately? Anyone *else* threaten you? "

"No!"

"Whether Iceman was responsible, this has to go back to Danny and his unsavory friends," Bryce said.

"My being attacked is *not* my brother's fault!"

"You don't know that, Hailey," Reilly said. "Danny got himself in big trouble here. You may not know the extent of it. Bryce has a point—the loan shark could have been proving that he has the upper hand. Or this incident could have been a warning to your brother by someone else."

Hailey gaped at them, looking from one brother to the other. "I can't believe you're both against him."

"No one is against Danny," Bryce argued. "We're trying to be realistic, that's all. I find it impossible to believe *you* made an enemy. Well, other than Danny's loan shark." Mattie had called her an angel, and it was true. Everyone liked her, so he had to look elsewhere for motive. "I want to make sure you're safe."

Bryce couldn't ignore the fear that somehow he'd brought the family curse down on her. How could that be, though? He cared about Hailey, was attracted to her, but that was far from being in love with her. More importantly, they hadn't done anything but kiss for effect so that Croft would buy their story. Surely his enjoying the act couldn't have put her in danger. No, the trouble had to stem from something Danny had done.

Reilly said, "I'll pay Iceman a visit, see what he has to say about his whereabouts."

"It's not like I have an address," Bryce argued.

"It's not like I don't have the resources to find him."

Reilly had always been competitive, had always fought with Liam to be in charge. Undoubtedly being a twin had set his nature. Ever since high school when Liam had left Lake Geneva to live in New Orleans with their maternal grandmother after their grandfather had died, Reilly had taken up fighting *him*.

This time Bryce let it drop.

"Listen, Hailey, while you're in Chicago,

don't go out alone," Reilly suggested. "At least not until we figure out who dumped you in the river."

"And in the meantime," Bryce added, "I'm going to get you out of here, take you back to Lake Geneva tonight."

"Bryce, no. You can't risk getting Croft angry just to get me home. You have that meeting with Croft in the morning. I know how important it is to you. Leaving can wait until after you're done."

Bryce scowled at Hailey. He was only trying to ensure her safety. "Can I count on you to stay put in the apartment until I get back?"

"Fine."

She sounded irritable, but he didn't blame her. And though she said it like she meant it, he didn't trust her. One call from Danny would undoubtedly send her running to her brother's rescue, thereby opening herself to more potential danger. Unless she had a guard.

Not that she would agree to one.

Not unless she didn't realize she was being guarded.

Knowing exactly what he had to do, Bryce

asked Reilly, "Can we get out of here now so we can go home and dry out?"

HOME. This wasn't her home, Hailey thought as she reentered the apartment she'd so swiftly left less than two hours before.

"Why don't you take a hot shower, get into dry clothes?" Bryce said, his voice muted. "I'll order us something to eat."

"I—I couldn't. Not hungry."

"Then I'll make you some tea."

"Bryce—"

"Don't argue with me. Go. Get comfortable."

After tossing the keys and ruined phone onto a magazine so the water wouldn't ruin the wood of the coffee table, Hailey did as Bryce demanded, feet still squishing in her running shoes, stripping them off and then her still-wet clothing as she crossed the guest bedroom carpeting into the bath.

Shock had set in. She was acting by rote. Her mind wouldn't concentrate on anything.

By the time she got to the shower, Hailey was shaking again and not because she was cold. Even so, hot water pouring over her helped abate the fear.

She longed for home—her cozy and safe

two-bedroom cottage with its wraparound porch in the front and the three-season room in the back. While she didn't have a view of the lake, it was only a five-minute walk away, and her home was grounded in nature, the view from the porch or windows being dozens of trees and bushes and masses of beautiful flowers.

Here in this apartment, she would always be aware of the cold, unforgiving river below the living area windows.

Shuddering, Hailey thought about how close she'd come to dying.

Using a fragrant shower gel, she tried to strip away the lingering fear as she washed whatever microbes the river water had left on her skin. But no matter how hard she scrubbed, she couldn't rid herself of the knowledge that someone had tried to hurt her.

Or had he tried to kill her?

Surely Danny wasn't responsible—not for this.

Part of her wanted to call him and make certain that her brother wasn't involved in anything darker than gambling. That he didn't have someone else on his back who might get even for something Danny did or didn't do by taking out his sister. The other part wanted to believe in her brother, wanted to remember the good Danny, the one who'd taken care of her when their mother had left them because her new husband "hadn't signed up to take care of another man's family" when he'd asked her to marry him. That Danny would never put her in danger.

She wanted to believe in coincidence.

Done with the shower, Hailey dried herself and wrapped her hair with a towel. Then she donned the thick robe Bryce had left hanging on the bathroom door. Warm at last, she thought to join him. He'd put his own life at risk to save hers, and she still needed to properly thank him, but she didn't know how. Words simply were not enough. If she hadn't taken offense at what he'd tried to tell her about her brother, if she hadn't run out on him, she never would have been in danger in the first place.

What to do?

Although she was grateful to be alive, she couldn't think clearly. Exhaustion turned her limbs into rubber and her brain into mush. The bed was so inviting. Maybe if she just curled up on top for a few minutes, she would figure it all out.

The moment she set her head on the pillow,

though, her eyes fluttered closed and she was lost....

Sometime later, she heard a knock and then footsteps brushing the carpeting and finally a softly whispered, "Hailey?"

Feeling as if she were floating in a dream, she couldn't seem to open her eyes. She sensed someone standing over her...heard a clink on the nightstand...smelled the inviting fragrance of a spicy tea...knew when he leaned closer...felt his lips brush her cheek.

"Sleep well."

Instinct turned her and before Bryce could retreat, she sleepily snaked her arms around his neck. "I need to thank you for saving my life."

"You're welcome."

He started to pull away, but she didn't let go.

"You don't understand..." Pulling herself up against him, she hugged him tight, then kissed him. "Really, I need to do more than say the words."

And kissed him again, this time pouring her emotion—her gratitude at being alive—into the embrace. He struggled to free himself, but she wouldn't let go. She needed the contact, the proof that she was very much alive.

Groaning, he finally gave in and swayed down into her, pushing her back against the bed. The robe opened and he lay against her bared flesh.

"Hailey, this isn't a good idea."

"I need to thank you…to feel normal…"

Heat curled through her and she pressed her hips upward until she felt him harden against her flesh. Eyes closed, she rubbed herself against him, then moved his hand down her side and over her leg to the vee between her thighs. Hesitating only a second, he explored her wet warmth.

Incredible sensations flowed through her. She moved against his hand, couldn't undo his pants fast enough. He was stroking her now, his fingers inside her echoing the rhythm of his tongue in her mouth. She wanted this… wanted him…wanted to prove that she was still alive.

Ready for him, she freed him from his clothing and led him to her opened thighs.

"Not yet," he whispered, placing one hand over hers and showing her what he wanted her to do to him.

Hailey flushed as she manipulated him, his

quick intake of breath exciting her as much as his exploring fingers. She watched his face, waited for his expression to change, anticipated the moment he was ready.

The immediate pressure at her entrance was sweet and life-affirming. Exactly what she needed, what they both needed, she thought as he pushed against her, and she pulled at his hips until he went in so deep that he filled her.

Needing him…needing every sensation that she could gather…she rubbed her breasts against his chest…wrapped her legs around his hips and lost herself in the act as he moved faster and harder until he brought them both to climax. Every inch of her flesh shuddered with release.

It was only after she floated down from the high, his weight pressing her into the bed, that she realized that while sex made her feel alive, it didn't make her feel any safer.

She had to be honest, had to admit that someone had tried to kill her tonight.

What if he tried again?

## *Chapter Six*

"My brother and one of my best friends get married and don't even invite me to the wedding? What's up with that?" Grania McKenna demanded after Hailey opened the door to Bryce's apartment the next morning.

"Spur of the moment?" Hailey threw her arms around Grania who hugged her back, then, expression puzzled, pulled away to take a better look.

"I didn't even know you two were seeing one another."

"We weren't."

Grania frowned. "Then Bryce was serious when he said the marriage was strictly business?"

"Business for him, personal for me," Hailey said, pulling her friend inside and closing the door. "Bryce saved Danny."

Grania looked every bit a McKenna with

spiked short auburn hair that set off her creamy complexion, freckled nose and sparkling green eyes.

"Danny? What does he have to do with anything? I don't get it, Hailey. Bryce said you were married yesterday, then you had some kind of trouble last night and that now you needed a friend."

Had he now? What was Bryce up to? Hailey wondered.

"Did the two of you have a fight or something? On your wedding night?"

"No, not exactly."

Hailey hoped Grania didn't bring up any intimate questions. As it was, after last night, she could hardly look at Bryce. She'd forced herself on the man and then had fallen asleep again. When she'd awakened at dawn, he had already escaped to his own room. Now they were both acting like nothing had happened between them. Nothing really had, she told herself, other than a physical release they'd both needed. They'd had gratitude sex. That's all it had been.

"Grania?" Bryce called from the kitchen. "Come on in. Coffee's ready."

"Doughnuts?" Grania asked, sweeping past Hailey.

"Of course. I know what puts my little sister in a good mood."

Grania looked back. "I want details. All of them."

Not knowing what exactly her new husband had told his sister, Hailey hid her discomfort. "I think you'd better ask Bryce."

"Now that doesn't sound good at all."

Grania made no bones about getting the details from Bryce. And Bryce didn't seem in the least uncomfortable admitting he married Hailey to get financial backing from James Croft and in return paid off Danny's gambling debt.

"I don't believe it! How could you?" Grania demanded of him.

"We're both adults."

"Marriage is supposed to be about love and commitment."

"I *am* committed."

"For the wrong reason!"

"Thank you for your opinion, but it's my life." Bryce moved closer to Hailey and slipped an arm around her shoulders. "Our lives."

Grania stared at Hailey, who itched to move away from Bryce. She kept getting hit with flashes of the things they'd done to each other

the night before. The things they would probably never discuss. Or do again, more was the
pity.

"Hailey, why didn't you tell me about
Danny needing money?" Grania asked. "I
would have helped you figure something out."

"Danny called when I was at the party for
Croft the other night. Bryce found me right
after the call. I was so upset. I had no idea of
how I was going to put my hands on a hundred thousand dollars. Bryce came up with
the solution."

"A hundred thousand…?" Grania aimed
her disapproval at her brother. "So you *forced*
her to marry you?"

"He didn't force me to do anything," Hailey
said, remembering the way Bryce had made
her touch him. She felt her ears grow hot.

"Then what do you call it?" Grania asked.

"A business deal," Bryce said. "Many mar-
riages are based on something other than love,
finances being the most common reason."
He checked his watch. "Speaking of which,
I need to get to a meeting. I'll be gone for a
couple of hours. Will you be here when I get
back?"

His sister stared at him. "I guess I will."

"You don't have to stick around if you don't

want to," Hailey told her, glaring at Bryce. She knew exactly what he was up to. "I don't need a babysitter."

"What am I missing here?" Grania asked.

"Hailey almost drowned last night. An attacker threw her into the river and I had to go in after her."

"What? Who?"

"We don't know, but Reilly's on the case. I have to go or I'll be late."

He gave Hailey a swift kiss on the cheek, making her heart thud the moment his lips touched her flesh. Her mouth wanted the feel of his, the fullness of his tongue inside. The fullness of his sex inside her, too.

Bryce said, "Don't let her get you into any trouble."

Did he mean her? Or Grania? Whichever... Hailey flushed at the bawdy thoughts she couldn't keep at bay. Kissing his sister on the cheek the way he had her, Bryce swept out of the room. Seconds later, Hailey heard the front door open and close.

Taking a big bite of doughnut, Grania washed it down with a swallow of coffee. Then she said, "I don't even know where to start."

"Pick something."

"This marriage. How could you do it?"

"I had to. For Danny."

Grania shook her head but didn't say anything. Hailey was certain her friend wanted to give her the tough-love speech, but for a woman who normally put everything on the line, Grania was holding back.

Finally, she said, "I can't believe Bryce. If he wasn't my brother, I would—"

"Don't blame him. I'm so grateful that he helped Danny out of a tough spot. If Bryce hadn't come up with the money, I would have had to sell my house. If I could have."

"Bryce could have loaned you the money."

"He didn't owe me anything, Grania. As far as a loan is concerned—" Hailey shook her head "—I couldn't have accepted. This way we both got something we needed." She poured herself a cup of coffee, saying, "I understand why Bryce wanted a wife right now…but I don't understand why he said he would never marry for love."

"I told you about the prophecy."

"Come on, Bryce doesn't seem like the kind of man who believes in curses."

"Bad things have happened to the McKennas, Hailey. To us. Mom just left the house one evening never to be seen again. She vanished into the rainy night. Dad hired private investigators, but they never got a lead on where she might have gone. There was no trace of her or of her car, and Bryce took it the hardest. He felt responsible."

"Responsible? How?"

"I don't know. He was away at school, so what could he have done? He would never explain. Maybe it has something to do with his being the oldest. He has always taken on extra responsibility for all of us. What I do know is that he was brokenhearted and swore he would never marry, would never fall in love, because he never wanted to be responsible for putting someone else in danger."

A fact that softened Hailey toward Bryce. She'd been angry with him because of his attitude toward Danny. She'd thought family was simply not important to him. She'd been wrong.

What else had she been wrong about?

JAMES Croft was already waiting when Bryce entered the restaurant.

"Well, good morning," Croft said, shaking Bryce's hand. "You look like you've had a night full of action."

Thinking Croft had somehow found out

about the river incident, Bryce said, "You know what happened?"

"I have a good idea. It might be years since I got married, but I still remember I didn't sleep much that first night."

*A woman who looks like that—he's crazy if he slept at all.*

Bryce forced a smile when he heard Croft's thoughts concerning bedroom action. Indeed, that had taken up most of Bryce's night. Not the doing, which had been spectacular if short, but the hours afterward he'd spent torturing himself. He'd never meant to break his pact with Hailey. Apparently she'd been feeling needy after the scare she'd had, and he had gone right along with it. She would be all right, he told himself. He wasn't in love with her. She was safe from the prophecy. Neither of them had spoken of what had happened between them, and he'd felt a little awkward around her this morning. Hopefully, an apology would ease the tension.

Realizing Croft was staring at him as if waiting for something, Bryce tried tuning into his thoughts, but as usual, he couldn't force the issue. He heard what he heard when the fates deemed. "Sorry, I guess I am a little worn out."

"No problem. I already ordered for us. I hope you are a steak-and-egg man. Red meat will give you energy."

"Sounds perfect." The man was so controlling, he even had to tell him what to eat. Hiding his irritation under yet another forced smile, Bryce opened his briefcase. "I hope you're in the mood to sign a contract."

He handed the packet to Croft, who barely looked at it before slipping it into his own briefcase. "I can do this later."

"I thought you would have a lot of questions for me."

"Let my lawyer look over the paperwork first. I'm sure he'll have a few."

"Then it's settled?"

"Nothing is settled until the papers are signed. Let's talk about something else."

Bryce clenched his jaw and hoped his frustration didn't show. He'd done everything he could to win over Croft. He'd even taken advantage of an old friend. And now Croft wanted to talk about something else?

"So when are you leaving for Lake Geneva?" the man asked.

"This afternoon," Bryce said. "Why? Can your lawyer expedite the process if I stick around for another day?"

"I don't think that's going to be possible. I have a few things to take care of tomorrow. And then I'd like to come back to Lake Geneva myself in a couple of days, have your new wife take me to look at some properties. Will she be up to that?"

Despite her experience and what had gone on the night before, Hailey had seemed to be herself that morning.

"I don't see why not," Bryce said.

"Including Widow's Peak?"

The man was obsessed with a place he'd never seen. What was that about?

"That would be up to Hailey."

"Did she get the Anderson brothers to agree to let her handle the sale of the estate?"

Seeing that the very idea lifted Croft's mood, Bryce said, "Things in real estate don't necessarily work that fast, but I'll do what I can to help speed up the process."

## Chapter Seven

"Croft wants to see Widow's Peak," Bryce told Hailey when they hit the outskirts of Lake Geneva late that afternoon.

Croft had been on Bryce's mind the whole drive, Hailey thought. Or maybe he'd chosen to talk about something that left no room for what had happened between them the night before. It was just as well even though she couldn't put it out of her mind any more than she could being thrown in the river. Every time she touched the cell phone he'd bought to replace her ruined one, she was reminded of what could have happened if Bryce hadn't followed her.

As difficult as it was to switch gears from almost drowning followed by her foolish seduction of Bryce, she had to get her mind back to her normal life, Hailey thought. And somehow, she put up a good front.

"I don't even know if the estate will be for sale yet," she said.

"You probably should call Ray as soon as we get back in town, see if he's talked his brother into letting go of the property."

"I'll make a follow-up call, certainly, but I don't want to pressure Mike. He was less than thrilled that I felt…well…*things* in the house."

"Felt what? You mean a spirit?"

His skeptical tone made her clench her jaw. She took a big breath and said "His aunt…*for one.*"

"There was more than one?"

A shiver shot through Hailey as she thought about how she'd had to force herself to go inside. "I sensed something dark and very scary the moment I stepped foot on the porch."

"Dark and scary how?"

"I think someone died there."

"That shouldn't be a surprise," Bryce said. "The house is more than a century old. Back in the old days, before we had so many hospitals, people died at home."

"True. This felt different somehow…I can't explain it."

"It's possible your mood affected you. Your

brother had just gotten a death threat and you were worried about him. That could have been preying on your mind."

"I hope you're right, Bryce. I hope nothing terrible happened at Widow's Peak in the past."

"If you find out it did, please don't share that with Croft."

Her jaw clenched again. Now he was trying to tell her how to run her business? That wasn't going to fly.

She couldn't help her stiff tone. "There's a little thing in real estate called disclosure."

"That applies to things like a furnace that doesn't work properly or electrical problems or black mold, not to stigmatization due to anything that happened on the property."

Bryce actually sounded indignant, Hailey thought. As if he had a personal stake in the issue. Which, considering James Croft's interest, she guessed he did.

She asked, "How would you feel if I sold you a property where I knew something terrible had happened and didn't tell you?"

"But you don't know anything about what might have happened at Widow's Peak for certain."

"I know what I sensed."

"What good would it do to tell Croft that other than make him think negatively about the estate? Maybe make him not want to buy it."

Maybe make Croft not want to sign with Bryce? Hailey frowned. Of course, Croft—his reason for fighting her on this. How far would he go to make this deal? She was beginning to think he cared so much about money that he would do anything.

"How does Croft even know the estate will be to his liking?" she asked.

"He won't know until he sees it. He wants what he wants and he usually gets it." Bryce's words were thick with tension. "So I would appreciate your doing whatever you can to make it happen."

"I understand you want Croft on board, Bryce, and I'm certainly willing to help you if I can, but surely if it doesn't go through, it's not the end of the world."

"The deal *has* to go through."

"Having money is great," she said, "but not when it changes a person so that that's all that matters to him."

Bryce didn't respond. Hailey sensed a shift in atmosphere. He closed himself off from her and focused on the road ahead. Suddenly she realized he'd gone straight through town and was heading for Williams Bay.

"Wait a minute!" Hailey protested. "You passed up my place."

"What, did you need to stop for something?"

"Um…it's my home."

"Not anymore."

"Bryce—"

"Married couples don't usually live in separate residences, Hailey."

"I like my house just fine," she informed him. "Moving in with you wasn't part of our agreement."

"If you want people to believe we're married, we need to act like we're married, which includes living together."

"You mean if *you* want *Croft* to believe it. He's the one you're worried about, right? But he wouldn't know where I was living. He's in Chicago."

"With plans to come back out here as soon as he can. He might be a little suspicious if you weren't at McKenna Ridge."

Hailey glared at him. He had a point, of course, and she wouldn't be so prickly about it if they hadn't just had a tiff. Or perhaps if they hadn't had sex the night before.

What had she been thinking?

Well, of course she hadn't been thinking at all, merely acting out of fear and gratitude, sheer emotions. She'd needed him to make her feel alive then, but now she couldn't allow herself to romanticize the act.

"Fine," she finally said. "But I want my own room."

"You can have any room you like. Don't worry, I won't force myself on you."

Hailey's cheeks flared with heat. Is that what he'd thought she'd done—forced herself on him? He certainly hadn't objected. At least not strongly enough to turn her away.

Once was enough for her. She didn't need to get more attached to Bryce McKenna than she already was. Even though she was grateful to him for saving Danny and then for saving her, she didn't like some of the insights she was getting from him. Better not to delve any further into a relationship that would surely end with him walking away when he had what he wanted, leaving her as had both of her parents.

BRYCE hadn't predicted that Hailey would take the lower level—of the four suites from which she could choose, these rooms were farthest from the master—but when she said that's what she wanted, he didn't object. Didn't she trust herself being closer to him? Bryce wondered as he carried her bag down the stairs. Perhaps she feared a repeat of the night before.

That wasn't his problem. Quite the opposite, actually. He hadn't been with a woman for a while, and Hailey had reminded him of what he'd been missing. Now that his libido had been kick-started, it was remaining in active mode. Every time he looked at his new wife, he wanted to have her again. Even in the middle of their disagreement, when he'd retreated, he hadn't lost his desire for her.

It was only natural, he told himself. They were, after all, married. And she'd started it. He'd been content to keep things platonic. Had been. Not now. What would be the harm? After thinking about it, he'd come to the conclusion that her being attacked the night before was either a random mugging as she seemed to think…or it had something to do with her brother. Not with him. He wasn't, after all, in love with his wife, so no matter what they did or didn't do, she would remain safe from the prophecy.

Unfortunately, with Hailey ensconced in

the suite farthest from his, it didn't seem as if the opportunity to follow up on the passion they'd shared the night before would present itself.

Leaving her bag on the bed, he hurried up the stairs to look for her. The family room door was open. Crossing to it, he stopped at the screened door. She was on the small patio directly outside. Cell phone to her ear, she silently stared out across the lake.

She appeared beautiful…enticing…annoyed…

"Hi, Ray, this is Hailey Wright. I'm back in town and will be in my office tomorrow. I'm going to look at comps and then figure out an asking price for Widow's Peak. I'll call you when I have something. Or you can give me a call back. Any time. Thanks." After leaving the message, she slipped the cell phone into her pocket, and as if sensing that he was standing there on the other side of the screen door, she glanced his way. "I did as you asked."

"So I heard. Thank you."

"I'll need a ride back to my place so I can get my car. And more of my things."

"You want to go right now?"

"Later. It's a perfect afternoon. I don't mind

spending it out on the patio. Maybe if I stretch out, I can nap. Not enough sleep."

"Sure. Later. We can have dinner in town. Then I can help you load up your car and follow you back."

"Whatever."

Bryce suddenly felt like they were an old married couple with little left in common other than polite responses. "If you want to take a dip in the pool, there are extra suits in the closet next to the powder room."

"Sounds like a plan."

With the distinct notion that she didn't want his company, Bryce took his own things upstairs and unpacked. Wishing he could read her mind as easily as he had at the river, he knew that wasn't going to happen. The ability taunted him. He had no control over it. There were times it was simply there. More often, he was simply tuned out.

As he unpacked, he found himself listening for Hailey moving around the house below. And then, when she did get out on the pool patio, he watched her from an upstairs window. The bathing suit she'd chosen showed off her curves to good measure. His physical reaction was instant, the night before replaying itself in his head. But there was no use daydreaming about what wasn't going to happen. It was obvious to him that Hailey regretted having had sex with him, probably regretted agreeing to his bargain at all if their disagreement over how to handle James Croft was any indication.

Perhaps he should have been straight with her. Without an influx of private funds, McKenna Development would go under. His father, who'd taken a backseat in the company and was already in semi-retirement, would be ruined financially if that happened. The old man might have to go out and find another job or lose his home. As would he and Grania. The only way to save the company was to get that outside money or to sell McKenna Ridge, which was impossible, of course.

The lake house was in a land trust and belonged to the whole family, including the twins. But Reilly and Liam had no stake in McKenna Development, so it would be unfair to ask them to sell off their heritage.

Beside, the lake house was the only thing they had of their mother. It had belonged to her parents, and as their only child, she'd inherited and had put it in trust for her children and her children's children. Breaking the trust—if he could—and selling the house even if his dad and siblings agreed would feel like a betrayal of her memory.

Bryce simply wouldn't consider it.

So getting Croft on board was their only hope. And to do that, he knew he needed Hailey's help.

"So what can I do to help?" Bryce asked when he pulled up to her cottage and parked early that evening.

Before he could take the keys out of the ignition, Hailey said, "Why don't you just go back to the house." Not used to being answerable to anyone—well, anyone but Danny—she could use a little alone time. "I don't have that much I want to bring over to the house, so it won't take me long to pack another bag, but I have some things I need to get together. Work related."

"Are you sure?"

"Positive. Don't worry, I'll be back at Mc-Kenna Ridge tonight in case Croft has someone spying on us."

"That isn't the point."

"Then what is?"

"I don't like your being alone."

"I'm fine here. I feel perfectly safe." This

was her home. Her haven. "Are you saying I'm not?"

"I don't know what to think after last night, Hailey. I'm just being careful."

Bryce sounded as if he did care, which he undoubtedly did in his own way. Hailey couldn't forget his coming to her rescue all those years ago. He seemed to be in possession of the rescue gene, but she was certain he wouldn't have to use it here of all places.

"Really, I'll be fine. I just need a little space."

"All right." He restarted the engine. "Call if there's anything I can do."

"Promise." With that, she exited the car. "Don't wait up for me."

Before he could protest, she shut the passenger door and escaped into the house. Closing the door behind her, she took the first deep, full breath she'd had since Danny's call. Her brother was safe. And here in her own home, no matter what doubt Bryce might have, so was she.

Her choice of decor was eclectic. Modern couches and upholstered chairs in plain fabrics, antique tables and buffet and desk. The house was about fifty years old—mid-century modern as they now called it—so she thought the combination of old and new fit it well. Unlike some people who bought the furniture with the house and never changed anything, she'd replaced everything in the living area and was looking forward to re-doing the bedrooms. When she had some money again. When this arrangement with Bryce was over.

Bryce…how was she going to stay married to him, considering the constant tension between them? Hailey wondered as she went through her closet for some essentials. She wouldn't pack much—she could always stop by here from the office to get anything she needed. Going through her lingerie drawer and handling her favorite lacy undergarments made her think of Bryce. Alternately angry with or attracted to him more than she'd ever been with another man, she wondered how they could live in the same house for months without something physical happening between them.

And if it did…that wouldn't be good for her.

That schoolgirl crush she'd once had for Bryce could turn into a future nightmare. What if she fell in love with him? Deeply and truly in love?

Bryce didn't want love in his life. He'd rather put all his energies into his business. Even knowing he had good reason to be cautious where love was involved—that for some reason he felt guilty about his mother's disappearance—she needed to protect her own heart.

So she skipped past the pretty lingerie and opted for more practical cotton.

That would keep her mind on the right track.

She hoped.

Bag packed, she wheeled it into the living area and then went out to the three-seasons room, which she used as her home office, even having a space heater so she could use the room in deep winter. Like the living area, the office was eclectic—antique desk, modern loveseat and lots of plants. She preferred using this for her office because of the wonderful views.

Besides, she never knew when Danny would show up and park himself in her spare bedroom.

Disconnecting her laptop from its docking station, she slid it and the wiring into a padded case, which she placed next to her suitcase. Then she took the watering can to the kitchen sink, filled it and brought it back to water her plants.

*Mental note: put watering on her online calendar so as not to forget.*

Reaching over the couch to water the final plant, a large ficus in an even larger planter on the floor, Hailey started when something moved outside the windows.

Pulse thrumming, mouth suddenly dry, she stared out into the dark. But if anything—or anyone—was there, she couldn't tell.

Still, even thinking there might be gave her the creeps.

Backing away from the windows, she shut off the lights all the way through the first floor. Then, breath held, she sat gingerly at the edge of the loveseat and simply waited for something to happen.

Five minutes passed. Another five. Soon she started feeling foolish. What had she been thinking? It could have been a stray dog. Or even a deer that wandered from a woody area too close to town. Whatever it was, she had nothing to fear.

Taking a big breath, she left the room, picked up her laptop case and wheeled her suitcase to the front door where the porch light assured her no one laid in wait. Nerves still needling her, heart thumping so she could feel it, she left the house and locked the door and got to her car at the curb within a minute flat.

After taking a quick look around to be certain she was alone, she placed the suitcase and laptop in the trunk.

Once she was in the driver's seat, door locked, engine started, she took her next big breath and felt her pulse slow. Wow, had Bryce kick-started her imagination!

It was only when she pulled away from the curb and checked her rearview mirror that her pulse fluttered once more when she saw another set of lights go on down the block behind her. Hands gripping the steering wheel, she headed for the center of town. The lights followed.

She turned on Main Street.

So did the lights.

No reason to be worried, she told herself. Just a neighbor or visitor who happened to leave at the same time she did. The other car would cut off on Mill Street or Center or Broad. Only it didn't.

Staying a generous distance behind, it nevertheless followed her through town and out onto the highway.

Hailey's hands on the wheel grew slippery with sweat as she kept glancing into her rearview mirror. What to do? She didn't want to lead the person straight to McKenna Ridge. So rather than waiting for the fast way to Bryce's place, she turned in toward the lake a couple of miles back. The long way would give her an extra mile or so of side roads to use if the other car followed, which it did.

Swearing under her breath, Hailey thought ahead and decided where she would turn. If she could do it fast enough, she could cut her engine and douse the lights and call Bryce for help. Hopefully, the other vehicle would speed by. But a glance into her mirror showed her the lights were now only half the distance back they had been and were closing fast.

Panicked, Hailey made a curve and a hilly area and then, forgetting her plan, turned on the first street away from the lake, hoping she could circumnavigate the maze of streets here and somehow lose whoever was driving the other vehicle.

This time, the lights didn't follow but kept going straight on the main road.

Braking, Hailey pulled the car over and put it in Park. Her whole body was shaking as she craned around just in time to see the other car pull into a lakeside estate.

She'd convinced herself she was once again a target.

She'd never been so thankful to be wrong.

## Chapter Eight

Bryce was pulling bacon and eggs from the refrigerator the next morning when Hailey came up from her suite.

"Good morning," he said.

"Morning."

She'd avoided him the night before, going straight to her quarters before he could ask if she'd like a glass of wine. He'd been disappointed, oddly so. He'd been looking forward to her company.

"Coffee," she muttered.

"Right here." He indicated the coffeemaker on the other side of the refrigerator. "Just made. I left a mug out for you."

"Thanks," she said as she slipped by him and poured.

She was already in a taupe summer pants suit, her long hair swept back in a clip, but the professional look didn't make her any less tempting. Then again, he'd been awake half the night thinking about her.

Taking a sip from the mug, Hailey groaned, the sound appreciative.

Bryce grinned. "I talked the Anderson brothers into having a late lunch with the two of us," he told her. "That'll give you enough time to get over to the office and find those comps."

"What?" Her gaze snapped to his. "Ray called back here instead of my cell phone?"

"Actually, I figured Mike was the one holding things up, so I called him last night. It took some convincing, but finally he agreed to at least hear what you had to say. He said he'd call Ray himself."

Hailey wasn't looking as happy as Bryce had expected her to be. Didn't she want the commission from Widow's Peak? Even if Croft decided he wasn't interested in the place, surely there was another buyer. A sale that big would certainly replenish her bank account. If she kept Danny out of it.

"Where and what time?"

"Ray's place at two, when the lunch crowd is gone."

"Fine."

"I thought you'd be a little more enthusiastic."

*At someone else taking over my job?*

"I'm not trying to take over anything, Hailey, I'm just trying to help."

She gaped at him, making Bryce realize he'd tuned in to her thoughts once more.

"My mistake, then." She found a travel cup in the cabinet and transferred the coffee from the mug into it. "I'm just going to take my coffee with me. I need to get to the office. I guess I'll see you at lunch."

"How about some breakfast first?" He waved the carton of eggs at her.

"For some reason, I'm just not hungry this morning."

He'd been looking forward to spending a leisurely hour having breakfast by the pool and their getting to know each other better. They needed to square away the tension that had kept them on edge, but it seemed that by calling Mike, he'd exacerbated the problem.

"Take something to eat with you in case you change your mind a little later. The refrigerator is still full with leftovers from the party."

"If I change my mind…" She stopped and

took a big breath. "Sorry. I'm just tired. And I have a couple of showings today."

"That's good, right?" Apparently things were looking up for her.

"I hope it's good. I've shown Mrs. Polder nearly a dozen properties, and none of them have sparked more than a slight interest. Maybe today will be my lucky day."

Hailey smiled at that and Bryce felt his gut tighten. Quickly covering his reaction to her, he said, "Okay, maybe I overstepped with the lunch thing. You don't need me there, so I'll bow out. You can say I had to take care of some business."

"You're sure?"

"Positive. What about dinner? Would you rather eat in town or here?"

"I don't know what time I'll be done." She headed for the door. "Go ahead and eat without me."

Bryce wanted to protest, to tell her he'd wait for her, but he would probably just make things worse between them, so he let it be. He didn't want her to feel pressured. Obviously she needed some time to adjust to the situation. Everything had happened so fast.

When she left the house, he stood by the

kitchen window, hoping she'd look back as she crossed the walkway to the steps.

She didn't.

Focused on her car, she went straight for it. Getting in, she turned it around and headed up the drive, all as if without another thought for him.

What the hell was wrong with him? Why did he feel so let down? Why did he suddenly feel…empty?

Maybe he was just tired of living alone. Eating alone. Maybe he just needed some company. That had to be it. He didn't need Hailey specifically. *Couldn't* need Hailey even though his thoughts centered around her whenever he wasn't obsessing over the business.

But how could he *not* like the woman?

She was attractive, hardworking, devoted to her brother. Too devoted, perhaps, so much so that she couldn't see Danny for what he was.

But Bryce understood and appreciated that kind of loyalty. She deserved that kind of loyalty in return, something that Bryce was willing to provide.

He would provide her with everything she needed if only she would let him.

Home. Business. Family.

Sex.

There was only one thing he would withhold from the relationship.

Knowing the fate of so many McKenna spouses and significant others—not knowing what happened to his own mother, for which he still blamed himself—Bryce simply wasn't willing to give Hailey his love.

"WIDOW'S PEAK has always been in our family," Mike Anderson said. "Maybe we shouldn't sell."

Hailey wore a smile that was becoming more uncomfortable as the meeting with the Anderson brothers went on. "Of course that's your choice." She wanted to shoot Bryce for pushing for this meeting.

They were sitting in the back of Ray's bar, beers and burgers on the scarred wood table, but she'd barely taken a bite, and she'd done that only to be polite. Getting food past the lump in her throat was nearly impossible. She'd prepared for the meeting most of the morning until she'd met with Mrs. Polder. As Hailey had come to expect, the woman hadn't liked the two homes Hailey had shown her, although she was anxious to view a third property that evening.

Nothing was going right today. Bryce should have left well-enough alone, but his mind was on a single track—make James Croft happy.

"Let's not be hasty," Ray said. "Selling the estate could be lucrative. Right, Hailey?"

"Yes, of course."

"How lucrative?"

"That depends. The property needs work if a potential buyer intends to live there."

"Which means putting out a lot of money." Now Ray was hedging. "Money we don't have."

His brother grinned at him. "How's this for an option? We could sell both of our places and then move in together."

"Yeah, the wives would like that."

Hailey saw her chance at a major sale fade away and tried to console herself that maybe the brothers would let her sell their individual houses if they went this route.

Mike argued, "The estate is big enough to house four families."

"If they didn't kill each other. Forget it. Not happening."

"Yeah, I suppose you have a point. I just hate to see it go out of the family." Mike turned to Hailey. "So how much do you think we can get for the place?"

"Like I said, that depends. If I put it on the market as is, you would most likely be attracting someone who would rip the place down to build a new mansion. I'm afraid you wouldn't get top dollar that way."

"We wouldn't want that!" Ray said. "As is…what do we need to do to get a buyer who would keep the old house?"

"You need to do repairs on the outside and at least some updating inside." She wasn't about to tell them about Croft's interest in the place, not until she had a contract. Then, if he followed up and insisted on seeing the estate right away, she would let him have a look to make him happy. She did owe that to Bryce. "Of course, the landscaping needs work and the rooms all have to be staged properly as well."

"What would that all cost?" Ray asked. "And how long would it take before we could actually put the estate on the market?"

"I don't know yet. I barely took a look the other day. I would have to take a more detailed tour of the place, to see what I think it needs. Then I would need to contact a contractor and get an estimate. I would guess renovations would take at least a couple of weeks. But any investment you put into the house will significantly increase the potential payout. More importantly, it will interest more potential buyers."

"And if we did everything you suggest?" Mike asked. "What would it be worth then?"

"I would say if it was in prime shape, I could list Widow's Peak in the neighborhood of three point five. Million."

The brothers looked at each other.

It was Mike who said, "How about letting us take a look at the contract?"

Relief flooded her as she opened her briefcase and handed each of the brothers his own copy. "The price is contingent on the work I feel necessary being done on the property, which I put in writing. If you want to sell as is, I would have to reduce the asking price significantly."

"What about your scaring off potential buyers?" Mike said. "No one wants to buy a haunted house. You need to keep that stuff about spirits hanging around to yourself."

Hailey looked from Mike to Ray who shrugged and said, "He's got a point."

"If that's what you prefer, of course."

But what happened if someone who knew

her reputation asked her specifically about any spirits in the house? Not wanting to turn the man off, she didn't ask.

As they read, Hailey found she could breathe easier.

"I don't know. I need some more time," Mike said. "I'm not finished going through Aunt Violet's things."

When Ray didn't say anything, Hailey reminded him, "The work will take a couple of weeks. You can finish looking through the place while the work is being done."

"I like to take my time. You never know what I might find."

Ray frowned. "Or what you won't find."

"All right. Then we'll give Hailey access to get the ball rolling. She can look around, decide what exactly needs to be done," Mike said. "What exactly it's going to cost us *before* we sign the contract."

Hailey tried not to let her disappointment show. "Okay with me."

"You have the extra set of keys?" Ray asked his brother.

"She doesn't need keys," Mike said. "She can come around and do her thing when I'm there."

"Mike—"

"Fine!" Mike reached into a pocket, pulled out a set of keys and slapped them down on the table in front of Hailey. "Stay out of my way and you can start poking around the place tomorrow."

ONLY Hailey couldn't wait until morning. After showing Mrs. Polder yet another property that had too many negatives for the woman, Hailey drove straight to Widow's Peak. She wanted to be able to get a feel for the house without having Mike Anderson breathing down her neck.

Obviously he didn't want to hear about spirits or someone dying in the place, but she couldn't forget the darkness that had enveloped her the first time she'd been inside. She needed to figure out what had happened there without an audience. That way she would have until morning to think about it, to figure out how best to handle the knowledge.

No surprises.

By the time she drove around the south side of Geneva Lake and entered the estate drive, the sun had set and dusk grayed the area. She passed several buildings on the property including an old horse barn, a storage shed and a multi-car garage. She would take a better look at them in daylight.

Her focus was the house and the weird vibes she'd sensed on Sunday.

Leaving the car on the drive, she stood for a moment, studying the outline of the main building, which was now deep in shadow. Wind whipped around her, no doubt the reason for the chill down her spine. Right now, the house simply seemed spooky.

Pulling out a recorder, she said, "Outside lights." Strategically placed lights would turn spooky into inviting. That's what she needed to do—to replace the negative with positive thoughts.

House keys in hand, she moved forward, stepped up onto the porch and once more hesitated as the horrible feeling of dread froze her in place and made her pulse speed up.

Confused as to why this particular spot had such negative vibes, she fought the weird feeling and took a good look around at the old-fashioned swing, flower boxes on the railing and a cast iron boot scraper and brush with a figural dog on the porch next to the door. The last was definitely an antique and had to be worth a couple thousand dollars.

More little details like that would add

charm to the residence if properly refurbished.

"Paint the outside, fix the broken window and install a new railing and flower boxes on the porch," she said into the recorder. "Paint the swing and add flower-print cushions."

Time to go inside. Her fear was in check, yet part of her regretted being alone. The only person she could imagine entering the place with her was Bryce. He would steady her and support her. He wouldn't judge, wouldn't call her crazy. He was a McKenna after all. One who could sometimes hear her thoughts and who believed in the hundred-year-old prophecy of a witch.

Steeling herself, she unlocked the front door and took a step inside.

The house was eerily quiet, the rooms still and gray. She flicked on the switch next to the door, but the single bulb above wasn't enough to dispel her uneasiness.

"Chandelier in the foyer," she said into the recorder, thinking she needed to check the lighting in each room. Buyers didn't like the idea of wandering around in the half dark.

A situation conducive to sparking her imagination.

But she wasn't imagining not being alone.

An eery sensation filled her. Her hands began to sweat and the recorder nearly slipped out of her grip. She shoved it in a jacket pocket as sorrow came at her in waves. Sorrow and desperation.

Because the spirit wanted something of her?

A scent teased her nostrils. Not violets. Not like in the upstairs bedroom. Not a single scent, but a light mixture of citrus and spice swirled around her and pushed at her as if it were trying to move her.

"I know you're here," she murmured. "Whatever happened to you…I'm so sorry. What is it you want of me?"

A shriek rent the air, making her whip around, but she saw no one. She felt the spirit, though…a very terrified woman.

The thought swept through her, filling her, frightening her, and was just as quickly gone.

"Are you still here?"

Maybe it was dust motes settling in the gloom, but Hailey imagined she saw movement in the middle of the nearest parlor… like a movie coming into focus. The breath caught in her throat and her stomach knotted. This wasn't something she'd ever experienced before. Normally she only *sensed* a spirit's presence, its emotions about a particular property. She'd never actually seen one. Apparently this spirit wanted to reach her.

The dust motes took form into a translucent figure. A woman with dark hair obscuring one side of her face, on the other side, blood running from her crushed forehead down her cheek onto her neck….

Hailey moved closer, but as quickly as she'd seen it, the apparition flickered out and was gone. The woman's presence wasn't. She pushed at Hailey's mind as if trying to make her face a knowledge that Hailey didn't want.

*The woman hadn't simply died here.*

*All that blood…surely she'd been murdered.*

That had to be the darkness she'd felt before and had tried to describe to Bryce.

The desperation Hailey felt was cloying, and she kept focusing on the word *help*. And if she wasn't mistaken—*here*. The woman was already dead, so how could she do anything to help? Hailey wondered.

*Here. Help…here…*

What did that mean? That the woman was killed here?

Creeped out, she moved into the parlor, hoping to figure things out. But while the awful feelings remained pervasive, they didn't clarify anything. How had the woman been killed? Had she been murdered with an object in this room?

Hailey began touching carvings and candlesticks and the poker still at the fireplace. Nothing "spoke" to her until she touched a heavy leather-bound scrapbook.

Before she could concentrate on the book or could open it to take a look, a sound that she swore was real, not just in her head, startled her. Was someone else here?

Quietly moving to the doorway, she poked her head around the corner but saw no one. She crossed the foyer, moving from doorway to doorway, parlor to library to music room to dining room. There she stopped and froze. Was she seeing another apparition in the gloom or was this man real? His back was to her, his hand slipping something into his pocket.

Then she recognized him.

"Danny, what are you doing here?"

Her brother whipped around to face her. Was that a guilty expression he wore?

"There you are, Hailey. I was looking for you, of course." He came to her and gave her a big hug.

As glad as she was to see him, she was also concerned over the circumstances. "How did you know I was here?" Or had he even been looking for her?

"I went to the office, and I saw the photos of this place and a preliminary copy of the contract that you drew up for the Anderson brothers. I know my little sister when she gets obsessed with something. Where else would you be?"

Hailey didn't know whether to believe him. Indeed, she might be obsessed by a particularly interesting property, but checking out a house at night wasn't something she'd previously done.

Danny had entered the house without calling out to her. He hadn't used the front door either. Did he know of another way to get in? Not only had he not tried to find her, but he'd also been pocketing something. Had he come to the house after dark to see if there was anything of value he could steal? Because she had no idea of what he'd had in his hand, Hailey couldn't bring herself to accuse Danny of theft.

Instead she asked, "What was so important that you couldn't wait until I got home to talk to me?"

"Which home? I wasn't sure where you would be tonight. I thought I would try to catch you at work. I wanted to make sure it was okay for me to still stay at the house."

"You're still my brother, aren't you? Of course it's okay." Hesitating only a second, she said, "Why didn't you call out for me when you got here?"

"It's a big place. I was just trying to use my cell to call you when you found me."

Is that what she'd seen—him slipping his cell back into his pocket? "My cell didn't ring."

"I couldn't get a signal."

That still didn't explain why he didn't simply call out for her, but she relaxed a little. Besides, she didn't want to argue. She wanted to tell her brother to go to her place now so she could continue investigating, but Danny's arrival seemed to have chased away the spirit.

"It's dark, so there's not much I can do here. The whole place needs a lighting upgrade. We should leave."

"Okay with me."

Danny led the way out the front door. Hailey paused in the foyer a moment before following. Even though she tuned in for any last messages, the house suddenly felt vacant—normal—like she hadn't made any connection at all. Like that poor woman hadn't been murdered.

Or was the truth even darker? she wondered, her imagination suddenly soaring.

Could it be?

Her heart nearly stopped when it came to her.

What if the woman's body was still here in the house somewhere?

## Chapter Nine

Hailey was glad to have a reason to leave Widow's Peak for the time being. Once she stepped foot off the porch onto solid ground the wind whipped around her, she felt like she could breathe normally again. Her investigation could wait—she'd had enough for one night.

"So what made you come back to Lake Geneva?" she asked Danny.

"Lack of funds." He shrugged. "I figured it would be easier to get work here where I know people rather than in Chicago. There I only know guys like Iceman. I doubt that you'd like me working for him."

Hailey shuddered. "Good that you came home, then." Maybe she could talk him into taking that job Bryce had offered him. "Did you have dinner yet?"

"No, I figured I would raid the fridge, assuming that was okay with you."

"We'll raid it together." Suddenly realizing hers was the only vehicle on the drive, she looked around, but it was too dark to see very far. "Where did you park?"

"Um, I didn't drive. I'm low on gas."

"You walked?"

"I borrowed a boat."

Hailey hoped she could take the word *borrowed* literally. Thanks to Bryce, she was now questioning everything Danny said.

"All right." She stood on tiptoe and brushed a kiss across his cheek. "Meet you back at home."

"Race you."

"No racing tonight. Just get there safe, okay?"

"Anything for you, sis."

A familiar reassurance. How many times had Danny said that to her over the years? After their mother had left them, any time she'd asked him for something, whether it was for money or help of another kind, Danny had always said, "Anything for you, sis." And he'd always come through. She'd never asked him where the money had come from, but now she wondered. Had he actually changed or had he always been reckless, maybe getting money in ways that weren't always on the up-and-up. Or even legal.

By the time she got back to the house, she was determined to be positive with Danny. It had been a while since she'd spent any time with her brother. Too bad about the circumstances.

Too bad her refrigerator was nearly empty, too.

Poking her head inside, she found Italian sausage in the meat drawer. Then, from a cabinet, she pulled a bottle of spaghetti sauce and a package of tortellini. This would make enough for dinner for both of them tonight and lunch for her brother the next day. Danny had hollow legs and he'd already said he was low on cash. She didn't care whether Bryce approved, she wasn't going to let her brother starve.

So when he walked in the door after she'd gotten a pot of water heating on the stove and the sausage broiling in the countertop oven, she said, "You're going to have to do some grocery shopping tomorrow." She pulled two twenties and a ten from her wallet. "Here's enough to get some groceries and put a couple of gallons of gas in your tank so you can get around town."

"I thought you weren't helping me anymore."

Bryce had been the one who'd said that, but she didn't want to bring him into this. "I'm helping *me*. I'm planning on having lunch here if I'm at the office. And if you don't have gas, how are you going to look for work?"

"Listen, Hailey, I really am going to look here in Lake Geneva. It's better I stay away from Chicago, at least for now, but if I can't find a job on my own here, if Bryce is still willing to give me work on his new project, I'll take it. I'm going to clean up my act this time."

Hailey only wished that was true. She hadn't wanted to believe Bryce when he'd told her he'd "heard" Danny think otherwise. But she wasn't a fool, just a sister who desperately wanted her old brother back.

"I might be able to help you with the work thing. If the Anderson brothers are on board doing some renovations on Widow's Peak before putting it on the market, maybe they can hire you. There's a lot to be done."

"I'm not a skilled laborer."

"You know how to use a paint brush. And gardening tools. And a bucket and a mop—"

Before she could finish, the sound of boiling water hitting the stove sent her running back to the kitchen. Dang, just as she'd been getting started.

A quarter of an hour later, when they sat down to eat, Danny said, "So tell me more about Widow's Peak. What kind of things need to be done there."

Hoping that he wasn't just trying to con her, Hailey began telling him about the house and the things that needed doing.

Leaving out her ghostly experience.

And her almost being drowned in the Chicago River.

It was nearly ten o'clock when Hailey headed for McKenna Ridge. She didn't know why she hadn't told Danny about almost drowning. She didn't want him to blame himself. If *this* Danny would. He hadn't even asked about her wedding or her new husband or her plans for the future. He'd acted like nothing had changed, even when he'd hugged her as she'd left her own house.

Surprised that Bryce hadn't called her, she was also pleased that he was giving her time to adjust to their new relationship. Perhaps she should have breakfast with him in the morning and try to get things on track. Or perhaps they could have a nightcap and talk things out, get to know each other better.

She really owed him so much both for Danny and for herself, and she hadn't been properly appreciative.

Why was it that Bryce could so easily push her buttons when he'd done only good things for her? What was that all about?

He was the same person he'd always been, one she'd always liked. She needed to keep that in mind. If he said or did things that disappointed her, perhaps she was expecting too much of him…just as she expected too little of her own brother.

No one was perfect, but most people had good in them. She simply needed to concentrate on the good in Bryce. Not that wanting to make a lot of money was bad. She was simply in a weird situation and with her and Bryce being at odds over Danny, she was probably being too critical of his every move in trying to make that deal.

When Hailey turned onto the long drive downhill, she noted Bryce's SUV wasn't the only vehicle outside the garage. A BMW sat next to it. Who was visiting so late? she wondered.

She didn't have long to wonder. Upon opening the door, she heard voices drift from the family room toward her. One, as expected, belonged to Bryce. And decidedly unexpected, the other voice belonged to James Croft.

Hailey groaned and wondered if she could sneak down to her suite without being detected, and then she called herself a coward for even considering doing so. Bryce had come through with his half of the bargain and saved her brother's life. On the other hand, while she had married Bryce to bring Croft on board, it seemed she had a way to go to make that happen. So she passed up the door to her downstairs suite and entered the family room instead.

"Hailey, there you are."

Aware of the tension in Bryce's voice, Hailey wondered what they'd been discussing. Had Croft shut down Bryce's project? Smiling brilliantly, she crossed the room, bent over to brush her lips across her husband's, ignoring the way her pulse picked up at the brief contact, and faced James Croft.

"Well, hello. What a surprise."

"A happy one for you."

A bit taken aback, she said, "Of course I'm always glad to see Bryce's business colleagues."

"No, I mean *for you*. I'm so enamored of the area, I definitely want to buy on Geneva Lake and I'm giving *you* my business."

"Wonderful." Hailey tried not to sound too excited. "There are several properties I can show you in the area."

"I'm really interested in Widow's Peak. It has a certain cache, a history that I can get behind. I've been doing my internet research. I simply must have the place!"

How odd. He hadn't even seen the property. Surely he didn't mean he would buy Widow's Peak sight unseen.

"I don't have the contract yet, but I'm working on it," she said.

"So what kinds of impressions do you get from the place? Any spirits wandering around?"

"There are probably spirits wandering around any old residence," Hailey said evasively. It almost sounded like that might be a selling point for him. "I should know if I'll be handling the estate by the end of the week."

Croft frowned. "Why wait that long? Give the owner an offer for me."

"That's only two or maybe three days. Besides, we haven't come to a price point yet. It depends on whether not the Andersons want to invest in the property by renovating it first. Widow's Peak needs a fair amount of work—"

"Which I prefer doing myself," Croft said with a wave of his hand.

"I would guess the Anderson brothers are eager to make top dollar," Bryce said. "Which would mean their having the work done before putting it on the market."

Croft settled down a bit. "Perhaps I should talk to the Andersons myself."

Which meant he might go around her and cut her out of the sale, which was possible because the brothers hadn't yet signed the contract. Hailey tried not to panic. "Let's not be hasty. I will let Ray and Mike know that you're interested, renovations or not, and see what they say."

"Fair enough. I can let you have a couple of days."

Recognizing the threat for what it was, Hailey didn't thank him. She was getting a bad feeling about this.

Why was Croft so desperate to get Widow's Peak no matter the condition of the house? Hailey wondered. Because he wanted to tear down the old Queen Anne and redevelop the area by splitting the land into smaller lots and then building several new multimillion-dollar mansions? She hated the thought, but business was business. If he could get permission to chop up the land—she had no doubt his pockets were deep enough to see that was done—then it made sense, of course.

Did that mean Bryce's housing development company would be part of that particular project?

Surely someone with Bryce's connection to the area and the old lake houses wouldn't want to see a significant piece of the area history destroyed. If he were part of such a plan, Hailey would be sorely disappointed in him.

BRYCE was relieved when Croft finally left. "I need some fresh air," he said, pouring a glass of wine at the bar. He offered it to Hailey. "How about you?"

"Sounds good."

She took the wineglass from him and he

poured another. They went out to the small patio several steps down from the house.

The night was perfect. Cool but not cold. A breeze rustling the trees. And the moon was just peeking out from behind some clouds. It could be called romantic if he were in that frame of mind. Glancing at Hailey, Bryce thought it too bad they had so many points of disagreement. He wondered what it would take to remove any obstacles to the bedroom. Or to anywhere for that matter. The thought of taking her out here in the wave pool or on one of the lounge chairs made him restless. Once was simply not enough for him.

Bryce waited until she made herself comfortable in one of the cushioned chairs before saying, "I had no idea Croft was going to show up here this evening."

"You don't seem very happy about it."

"He can be tiresome," Bryce admitted. He leaned against the iron railing so he could face Hailey. Moonlight became her, made her skin glow a silvery blue, gave her a downright magical aura. "I thought Croft wanted to have a business dinner, but all he talked about was buying into the area, and more specifically Widow's Peak."

"Did he say why that property specifically?" *And why he's so interested in whether Widow's Peak is haunted?*

Although Bryce had been wondering about Croft's interest as well, he didn't respond to Hailey's thought lest he put her off again.

"Croft simply went on about wanting to start a family tradition like we have here at McKenna Ridge. He said Widow's Peak had to be the most unique estate around and he didn't want what everyone else had."

"Did he make you a believer?"

"To tell the truth…I don't know."

"He's very insistent."

"Like I said before, when James Croft wants something, he doesn't give up until he gets it."

*Great. He already creeps me out. A sale is a sale—I have to remember that.*

Hailey's thoughts made Bryce wish he had an alternative backer so they could both be free of the man.

"So how did your day go?" he asked.

"Mrs. Polder still didn't see a house she liked. I'm starting to wonder if she really wants to buy or if she's simply looking because she's bored and wants something to do."

"Sorry. And I'm sorry Ray and Mike didn't sign."

"I do think they're on board. I was honest with them and told them the price would depend on whether they did what amounts to a lot of work on the place. They asked me to make a list of what I thought was necessary and they would see the difference in return over trying to sell as is. Truthfully, it's very difficult to sell a property in that shape unless the buyer's intention is to tear it down. But that's not what Croft wants to do, right?"

Why was she looking at him so intently? He tried to read her thoughts, but he suddenly felt as if he were standing outside a closed door. He wasn't getting anything off her.

"As far as I know Croft wants to live in the house. If he has other plans, he didn't say so." Then again, the man had been acting strangely. Not exactly out of character, simply more intense than usual, as if he had some secret reason for wanting the house. "So you'll be at Widow's Peak tomorrow?"

She nodded. "I was there tonight. I wanted to delve further into that vibe that disturbed me on Sunday. I wanted to clear it up alone. Mike will be there tomorrow, and he doesn't want to hear about spirits or the feelings I get from the house."

"And did you clear it up?"

Hailey got to her feet and moved to the railing next to him and stared out to the lake. "Not exactly."

Turning around to join her, Bryce realized she was looking out toward Widow's Peak now. Not that it was visible at night. He got the distinct feeling there was something Hailey was holding back. Whatever it was, she was blocking him from tuning into it. Certain she would tell him when she was ready to talk about whatever it was, he didn't press her.

"So what now?"

"Now I get to tour the place with Mike looking over my shoulder."

"I might be able to help you with that."

"How?"

"Bring me along. I can distract Mike, keep him off your back while you work."

Hailey grinned. "I can see it now. But that's unfair to you. It's my problem. You'll be bored."

He wanted nothing more than to work side-by-side with her, to see her smiling at him like that all the time.

"Hey, we're a team now and I'm all for teamwork. Besides, I won't be bored. I've never been inside the place. I could help figure out the costs of the work you want the Andersons to do on the place. Renovation is my business after all."

Again, she gave him an odd look before asking, "You're sure about this?"

"Positive."

Her expression softened. "All right. Deal." She held out her hand for a shake.

One touch and Bryce was lost. As if an electrical current pulsed through him, making him act, he pulled her into his arms. "I prefer sealing the deal like this."

He leaned into Hailey and her eyes widened, but she didn't move away. Bryce brushed his lips over hers. Knowing he should leave it at that, he simply couldn't, not when she sighed and swayed into him. He slid his arms around her back, pulled her closer and deepened the kiss.

He didn't mean to take it any further.

Then Hailey pressed herself more firmly into him. His physical response negated clear thinking. His erection was doing the thinking for him and he rubbed against her to tell her so. Her response was a moan, and she slid one leg up around his thigh so that her weight pressed him into the iron railing in back and into the vee between her thighs in front, making all his blood rush to that one place that make him ache for her.

Wanting to feel her soft flesh, he slid his hands up under her sweater and easily undid her bra and found her breasts.

"Hell," he murmured into her mouth. "Let's get into the wave pool."

They quickly undressed each other, hands exploring. When she pulled down his trousers, she dropped to her knees, so she could run her tongue along his length and surround him with her lips. Tangling his fingers in her hair, he held her head and rocked his hips so that he plundered her eager mouth. Her hands were still exploring, her fingers curling around him, and as if she could sense exactly when he was about to come, she stopped and pulled away.

He tugged her up and into his arms, and kissing her, danced her all the way to the wave pool. By the time they got into the water, he thought he would surely explode. He lifted her and pulled her to him, sex to sex. Her legs curled around his hips as she sank along his shaft.

Shaking and fighting to stay the distance, he let her go so that her upper body floated back as if she were lying on a water mattress. He could see her face and touch her breasts as he moved inside her. He captured her nipples and worked them until she cried out with pleasure and moved her hips faster. Then he slid a hand between them and found her clit, stroking and pulling at it until she cried out again, her body stiffening.

Unable to hold on any longer, he came hard and fast.

She pulled herself up so she could kiss him.

He kissed her back, hard and deep.

For a moment, he lost himself in the softness of her body, in the sweet taste of her mouth, in the sense of possession gripping him when she snaked her arms up around his neck and clung to him.

For a moment, he imagined anything was possible with Hailey.

For a moment…

And then the moment was over because that feeling he got—the one that warned him when he was heading for trouble, reminding him of why he couldn't love her or why they shouldn't be doing this—took charge.

Sheelin O'Keefe's prophecy suddenly filled

his thoughts. Bryce pulled his head from Hailey's and pushed her free of him, his very soul wracked with pain. It was a physical sensation, though not one he could attribute to any particular body part. He ached all over for what he couldn't have…for what couldn't be.

Eyes wide, Hailey stared at him, her expression questioning, as if she were waiting for him to explain.

"I lost my head." Bryce tried to ignore the way his chest squeezed tight and his stomach knotted. "I forgot our bargain. Sorry."

Without saying a word, she spun around in the water and flew up the steps. Grabbing her abandoned clothing, she headed back inside the house, her flawless flesh silvered in the moonlight, making him ache to follow. Even though every instinct told him to go after her and apologize and take her straight to bed where he could make love to her throughout the night into the wee hours of the morning, Bryce held himself in tight check.

He had to stop this madness before it was too late.

Because no matter how much he wanted to deny his legacy, no matter how much he wanted to believe what they'd had was just sex, he was starting to feel far more than was safe for her.

## Chapter Ten

After tossing and turning half the night thinking about what had happened in the pool, Hailey overslept. A quick shower was all she allowed herself before throwing on tan dress pants and a matching boatneck sweater. Brushing out her hair, she swiped on some lipstick, grabbed her shoulder bag and rushed up the stairs.

Would Bryce still want to go to Widow's Peak after last night? she wondered, still upset at the sudden turnaround. She would have done anything with him if he had only asked. Had he merely been restraining himself to keep to his promise as he'd said?

She'd been hurt when he'd pushed her away, but perhaps he was fighting himself, trying to live up to his part of their bargain. She hadn't argued with him, hadn't told him she'd wanted him. Would he have changed his mind if she had? If she had admitted she was falling for him, would he have run the other way?

Confused and upset with herself as much as with Bryce, Hailey was decidedly uncomfortable at the thought of spending the morning with him. Part of her hoped he'd thought better of coming with her.

Apparently not.

The coffee was made. The counter was laid out with two small plates of food—bread, cheese, strawberries. Dressed in tan slacks and a white polo shirt, Bryce was obviously waiting for her. His plate was already half-empty.

Filling the travel cup with coffee, she said, "I overslept. I need to get going."

"Not before you eat something. And we're going together, remember?"

So he was still planning on coming with her. She popped a strawberry in her mouth and made an impromptu sandwich of the cheese and bread, wrapped it in a napkin and slid it into her shoulder bag.

Picking up her coffee, she said, "I can eat while I drive. We need to take both cars so I can go from Widow's Peak straight to the office."

"Then let's get on the road."

Trying to keep her mind from wandering to anything personal, Hailey led the way to the vehicles, and once inside her car, turned on a CD loud enough to blast away any unwanted thoughts about Bryce and their lovemaking from her mind. An impossible task, it seemed.

But the moment they left their vehicles on the Widow's Peak drive behind Mike Anderson's truck, Bryce put an arm protectively across her back and she was lost.

Then the front door opened and Mike looked from her to Bryce. "You here as a professional consultant?"

"Something like that." Bryce held out a hand and shook Mike's. "Plus I wanted to satisfy my curiosity. Old buildings are my life."

Again Hailey wondered why he lived in a high rise if that were true.

But Mike seemed to buy it. "Come on in and take the tour, then."

"I've seen the house," Hailey said. "Most of it, at any rate. How about starting up at the widow's walk and working our way down. I never got up there the other day."

"Widow's walk it is."

Mike took the lead up the staircase to the second floor. Hailey fell behind slightly, indicating Bryce should go ahead of her. The house felt alive again, yet when she glanced at the doorway to Violet's room, she felt no pull. Mike opened the doors to the stairs and went up. Brushing her so that she shook inside, Bryce gave her a hot look that told her he'd felt it, too, before following Mike. Quickly climbing the narrow steps up to the covered widow's walk, all wood including the railings, Hailey stopped dead at the top.

"Quite a view up here," Bryce said.

"Yep." Mike pointed to a spot across the lake. "There's your place."

Hailey wasn't looking across the way. She wasn't looking at anything. Instead, she was concentrating on the flowery scent that teased her…

Was Violet up here trying to tell her something?

She looked around. The widow's walk would hold half a dozen people at most. An antique mahogany bench with carved leaves decorating both back and front snugged up against the only wall, placed on the south side. An odd addition to the widow's walk. However, having been protected by the wall in the back and the roof overhead, the beautiful bench was still in credible shape. Hailey tried to imagine Violet sitting there for any length of time while looking out to the lake. Or perhaps while reading a book. The bench must have had some such purpose. With a cushion and a couple of pillows, it would make a perfect retreat.

"Well, what do you think, Hailey?" Mike asked. "Is this a selling point or what?"

She started and focused beyond the railings in three directions, past what were magnificent views of the lake and surrounding estates.

"The view is a *great* selling point, but the railings probably need to be replaced." She pulled her camera from her bag and took several shots, including one of the bench. Then she traded the camera for her recorder. "Widow's walk needs a safety inspection and a paint job. Plus a cushion and decorative pillows for the bench."

They went downstairs to the bedroom level and started with Violet's room. She pulled out her recorder. "The master bedroom is in dire need of fresh paint and new linens."

By the time they got to the third of the dozen second-floor bedrooms, Mike was squirming when she continued her observations.

"You gonna record everything that's wrong with the place?" he asked.

"If my doing so bothers you, I could take notes on my phone, although keying them in would take even longer."

"Either way, it's going to take forever to get through all these rooms."

"You could give Bryce the twenty-five-cent tour of the house while I make my notes, then do whatever it is you need to do around here."

"Not a bad idea. And if you run into Aunt Violet, just leave her be."

"Sure," Hailey said, wondering about his attitude. What made him so resistant to what he could view as whimsy.

"I'd like to see more than the house," Bryce said, turning to wink at her without Mike seeing. "I ought to take a look at the other buildings on the property, too."

Hailey's pulse sped up a notch, but she tried to ignore it. He didn't mean anything by it. Their marriage had simply been convenient for both of them. The sex, too, at least for him.

"Yeah, sure, we can check out the other buildings," Mike said. "And then we can have a couple of beers on the porch." He looked to Hailey. "Take your time."

"Good. I like to be thorough."

And she could use some time alone with the house. Good thing Bryce thought about those other buildings. The men began going through bedrooms at triple speed, while she continued to make her notes. By the time she'd made notes on all second-floor bedrooms and bathrooms, plus the kitchen, laundry and powder room on the first floor, the men seemed to have finished inside.

"Wait a minute," she heard Bryce say. "What about the basement?"

"What about it? There's no living space down there."

Hailey entered the foyer where they were stalled out just as Bryce indicated a radiator. "But there's a boiler."

"Yes, we should at least have a look at the mechanicals," she agreed, trying to ignore the sense of discomfort she always experienced in this area. "Not that I'm an expert, but I don't even know if your aunt or uncle ever had the electric converted from fuses to breakers."

"Breakers," Mike assured them.

"Good," Bryce said, "but we still should have a look."

"It's filthy down there. No one's touched the place for years."

Why was Mike so set against going down there? Hailey wondered. "We won't touch anything, then."

Bryce slapped Mike in the shoulder. "C'mon, it'll take only a few minutes."

"All right!"

Truth be told, Hailey could skip this one, but her sense of dread was growing exponentially the longer she stayed in the foyer, so she quickly followed the men through the mud room to a wall that housed a secret panel, and then down the stairs. Not that she was able to leave the dismaying sensation behind. Her unease festered as she entered the dank, dark and very creepy basement. A single lightbulb lit the area giving her just enough light to see the myriad spiderwebs.

"Told you there was nothing to see."

Rather than arguing with Mike, Bryce went straight to the breaker box and checked inside, then took a good look at the hot water tank and ended up taking a panel off the front of the boiler.

As quick as he was, Hailey couldn't wait to

get out of there. She shifted her gaze around the big open space, which was probably only half the footprint of the house. The walls seemed to be crumbling, one of the windows was boarded up and a pile of old bricks sat between two doorways.

She took out her recorder. "Basement needs an overhaul. New electric for lights and at minimum, masonry work and a paint job." Then she asked Mike, "Why the doorways?"

"One goes to the outside, the other to the old coal bin."

"Coal?"

"That would have been the fuel of choice, even in the fifties," Bryce said. "Done here. Everything actually looks like it's in good shape."

"Well, hallelujah!" Mike said, leading the way back up the stairs.

Hailey had to admit she was glad when she got back to the first floor. She continued on straight into the dining room, checking not only for things that needed to be done but also for anything that was obviously missing. She didn't want to think that Danny had just taken something that had belonged to Violet when she'd found him the night before, and she was relieved not to see anything obviously disturbed.

The men's voices faded. The front door opened. Mike was taking Bryce outside, which would leave her in the house alone.

She decided to go back to the widow's walk. Although she'd smelled the scent of violets, she hadn't gotten any kind of strong impression. No sense of darkness like she'd gotten the night before. Even so, she'd felt Violet—her spirit must have wanted her to see something. The men's presence had no doubt interfered with her sensing what that might have been.

After glancing out a window to see Mike on his cell phone walking away from the house, Hailey made straight for the staircase and the widow's walk.

But if Violet had a message for her earlier, it must not have been important enough to linger. To her disappointment, the only scent that teased Hailey's nose was a fishy smell coming off the lake.

BRYCE lingered near the front door for a moment. Mike was making a call to his sports supply store to check on a delivery. Apparently it was nearly impossible to get a signal in the house itself.

With Mike's attention elsewhere, Bryce slipped back inside. As Mike had speeded up the tour, Bryce had glimpsed something he wanted to check out.

A scrapbook in the front parlor.

His psychic ability had always been limited to hearing others' thoughts when it chose to kick in. And yet, when he'd touched the scrapbook, he'd sworn his fingers had tingled. Now sitting in one of the upholstered armchairs, he pulled the massive book onto his lap.

The contents surprised him.

Rather than a collection of family photographs as he'd expected to find, the book was filled with decades of Geneva Lake history—newspaper clippings and brochures and entertainment programs. Page after page was filled with glimpses of the past in Lake Geneva and Williams Bay and Walworth and Fontana—all the towns around Geneva Lake.

Why had he felt such an overwhelming need to come back inside and check the scrapbook? Bryce wondered as he turned page after page. Violet had been a recluse after her husband's death, so had this been her way of connecting with the outside world?

Nothing in the scrapbook seemed extraordinary.

Nothing until he got halfway through the book.

Then a sense of urgency made him turn pages faster and faster until he got to the newspaper clipping with the headline: LOCAL WOMAN DISAPPEARS.

This was it. This was what he'd been meant to find.

Pulse quickening, Bryce sat frozen staring at the article about his mother's disappearance. It detailed the police department's fruitless search and his family's grief at the loss, not to mention their frustration at not knowing what had happened to their loved one. Just reading it brought back that next morning when Dad had awakened them to tell them the news. He'd been sick then.

Sick with despair.

With grief.

With guilt.

He was sick now, as if he were reliving that awful day.

The photograph of his mother wasn't a professional portrait but a snapshot of her in a happy moment. Lush dark hair spilled around Mom's face to her shoulders, and her smile was radiant. Posed in front of a flower bed, she wore a white, lace-edged blouse and a fine chain holding four tiny birthstone wheels—one for each of her children. Bryce remembered the present he and his brothers and sister had bought for her that Mother's Day, the very day Grania had taken this photo.

Bryce knew he'd returned to the parlor so that he could see this…but why?

How?

What could possibly have drawn him back to the scrapbook?

"Looking at Violet's photos?" Hailey asked as she came downstairs and saw Bryce staring at the scrapbook in his lap.

Bryce shook his head. "Come take a look for yourself."

Considering she'd been on her way to do that very thing, Hailey quickly took in the article about his mother's disappearance.

Her mind flicked to the other night, to the translucent figure she'd so briefly seen among the dust motes.

Could it be?

She sat on the chair arm next to Bryce as he continued to page through the scrapbook. There were several more articles about Alice's disappearance, the articles getting less and less space as the search for the missing woman ground to a halt. Then the contents changed tone, once more reflecting happier events in the area. Normal, everyday things. As Hailey continued turning pages, the sense of urgency waned only to be amped up when he went back to the first article with the photograph.

Staring at Alice McKenna's long dark hair, Hailey let the uneasy thought gel. What if the spirit she'd glimpsed so quickly *had been* Bryce's mother?

"Everything in this book is about an event that happened in this area." Bryce's intake of breath was audible. "Why would she have these articles about my mother?"

"I don't know." Not for certain. She was only guessing at something so awful she couldn't voice it, at least not yet. "Was your mom good friends with Violet?"

His dark expression made her want to put her arms around him and let him lean on her.

"Mom and Violet? Not that I know of. I never saw them together or anything. Then again, I was away at college that last year, so I'm not sure."

He sounded defensive…

Before she could probe a little, she heard footsteps on the porch. Regretting not being able to finish this conversation with Bryce, Hailey vowed to do it later. He quickly closed the book, returned it to its table just as the front door opened. Later, she would tell Bryce everything. By the time Mike entered and spotted them, they were on their feet and she was looking around as if for faults that needed to be addressed.

"So are you done?"

"Not quite. I still have a couple of rooms on this floor to go through."

"What do you think?" he asked Bryce.

Bryce started, as if he were just jerked out of his own private thoughts. "About what?"

"About how much getting this place in shape is going to cost me." Mike was sounding exasperated.

Hailey said, "I'm not even finished looking." Had he really thought they could figure it out on the spot? "After which I have to make a written list of everything I believe the property needs, so that nothing is missed."

"Then Hailey and I will put our heads

together," Bryce said. "Give us a few days to get a proposal together."

Mike scowled. "I'll get those beers."

"And I'll get back to work," Hailey said.

"I take it you didn't run into any ghosts," Mike said as he headed for the kitchen.

"Not today." She turned to Bryce, who still wasn't himself. "Are you okay?"

"Yeah, sure."

But he wasn't looking at her. He was lost somewhere in the past. His expression was odd.

He looked…guilty.

## Chapter Eleven

Thinking about Bryce's reaction to the articles about his mother in Violet's scrapbook, Hailey regretted his pain. What she didn't regret was not telling him what had happened to her the night before. Then he would be thinking the same thing she was, that the woman killed in the house had been his mother. She would have to tell him that.

Eventually.

She had a lot to think about before she opened old wounds again.

Rather than going straight to the office, she decided to stop at home to see how Danny was doing. Hopefully he'd gotten the groceries. It wasn't that she was stopping to check. It wasn't that she didn't trust him with her fifty dollars. It really wasn't.

Trying to convince herself of that, she turned onto her block and saw two men on her porch. She took her foot off the accelerator and let the car slow to a crawl. Both men were familiar. One was Danny, of course.

The other was Iceman.

Her pulse began to race. What was the loan shark doing here in Lake Geneva?

She hadn't forgotten Bryce's theory that, whether he knew it, Danny had something to do with her being dumped in the river. And Reilly had said he was going to have a talk with Iceman.

Is that why the loan shark was here, to threaten Danny because the heat was on him?

Only when he drove off did she give the car some gas and pull up to her house. Danny had already gone back inside. She gripped the steering wheel for a moment to steady herself. Then she left the car and went to face her brother.

She found Danny in the kitchen, putting food away in the fridge. That he had bought food with the money she gave him made her feel a little better. Now if only he an explanation for his visitor.

"What was Iceman doing here?"

"You saw him?"

"He was leaving as I drove up. What did

he want, Danny? Did he threaten you again? Or did you invite him here?"

"No! Neither one. He came to find me because he figures I have new resources."

"What?" Now he had her address, which didn't thrill her.

Danny said, "His words, not mine. He's trying to get me in a big-stakes game. I told him I'm not interested."

"Is that the truth?"

"What do you want me to say, Hailey, that I don't want to gamble anymore? That the urge is gone? It's not. I have to fight it every minute. But I didn't invite Iceman to Lake Geneva. He came looking for me. I told him that I'm not planning to get in this game. I'm trying to change. *For you.* I even have a job interview on Friday."

"With who?"

"Ray Anderson. He's short a bartender."

Thinking that would only be another temporary job with no payoff for the future, Hailey kept that opinion to herself. Work was work. If Danny got the job, that would be a step in the right direction.

"Good," she said. "Then I'm happy, Danny. I just don't want to see you get yourself in trouble again."

"I won't!"

"Iceman didn't make any more threats, did he?"

"Not this time."

She hesitated only a second before asking, "What about in Chicago?"

"What are you getting at, Hailey?"

"Something happened that I didn't tell you about."

Danny's brow furrowed. "When?"

"An hour or so after Bryce gave your loan shark the money, I went out for a run along the Chicago River. There was a car following me. Then a man wearing a ski mask got out and grabbed me. He was too strong for me to fight off. He threw me into the water."

"What?"

"I don't know if he intended to kill me, but if it wasn't for Bryce, I probably wouldn't be here today. I don't know what happened, Danny, but I couldn't fight the current. Bryce jumped in and towed me to shore."

"Another reason to thank him," Danny said, taking Hailey in his arms for a big hug. "Why didn't you tell me this before?"

"I figured you had enough worries."

"You're my main worry, sis. You always have been."

This was the Danny of the past, the one who'd always been there for her, who'd done what he had to so that she would be safe and happy. Hailey blinked away tears and rested her head on her brother's shoulder for a minute.

"Any reason you think Iceman was responsible?" he asked.

"I don't know." Hailey pulled away. "I don't know anyone in Chicago. It could have been him. Or someone else who has a grudge against you?"

"No one. I swear! Iceman is the only one I owed, and it doesn't make sense that he came after you because you arranged for him to collect. Are you sure someone doesn't have a grudge against you?"

"Not that I know of."

"No one you ticked off? A client, maybe?"

Hailey tried to think of anyone she'd put off. "Mrs. Polder? I can't seem to find a house that she likes."

"You think she could have thrown you in the river or hired someone to do it because you couldn't find her a suitable house?" he asked, irony rich in his tone. "What about your other clients?"

"What other clients? I've been in an increasing dry spell, Danny." And then it hit her. "Unless…"

"Who?"

"James Croft." The man had struck her wrong from the first. "I told you he needed Croft's financial backing for that new development—the reason we made our deal. Bryce brought Croft to McKenna Ridge and Croft wants to buy on the lake. Specifically he wants me to get him Widow's Peak, and he's not happy that I can't instantly give him what he wants. Come to think of it, Croft was in Chicago when I got dumped in the river."

"So you think he tried to drown you to convince you to get him the property?"

"Okay, maybe not."

"You sound like you have a problem with him."

"I think he only wants to buy Widow's Peak to tear it down and build a new development—a condo complex or several multi-million dollar homes. If so, there goes one of the original treasures on the lake."

"Wait a minute," Danny said. "Croft… Croft…" He paced the room. "I know that name."

"You might have read something about him in a Chicago newspaper."

"No, I mean from here."

"Last weekend was the first time he was in the Lake Geneva area."

"Are you certain of that? I swear I know that name from back in the day."

Why that possibility should bother Hailey she couldn't fathom. But when she got to her office, the first thing she did after returning a couple of phone messages and checking her email was to call her old boss. Mattie Sorenson had not only owned and run her own real estate agency for nearly forty years, but she'd also been on the board of directors of the Lake Geneva chamber of commerce. Mattie had closed shop and had retired the year before because she'd declared she was too old to fight the economy, but she always liked to hear what Hailey was up to.

"Hailey, honey, how are you doing? I heard you married that gorgeous Bryce McKenna. Congratulations!"

"Thanks, Mattie."

"You'll have to tell me all about it over lunch. That's why you called, right?"

"I would love to have lunch as soon as my life settles down. Maybe in a week or two?"

"You just let me know when. So what's up?"

"I have a new client, a buyer. I want to get the lowdown on him if there is one." Quickly she added, "You know, just in case it helps me figure out how to sell him. I thought he was new to Lake Geneva, but Danny seems to think he knows the name."

"Which is?"

"James Croft."

"Croft? Yes, of course. He was at Bryce's party. And I remember the Crofts from years ago. They rented a house on the lake for a couple of summers. I know because I handled the rental."

"How long ago was this?"

"Mmm, the last time had to be in the last century," Mattie said with a laugh. "I know it was more than a dozen years ago. There was some kind of trouble with one of the sons, and the family left in the middle of their rental and never returned."

"What kind of trouble?"

"Sorry, honey, that escapes me. My memory isn't as good as it once was."

Thinking that was all she was going to get from Mattie, Hailey shifted the conversation to one more personal, then set a date for lunch before she hung up.

But she couldn't let the Croft connection go...

WHY had Violet Scott kept those articles about his mother's disappearance? Bryce wondered on the drive home. Before leaving Widow's Peak, he'd had a few minutes alone to take another look at that scrapbook. Most of the articles had been about happenings in the area—not on individuals—so why had she been so focused on his mother?

Had Violet known what had happened to his mother that rainy night?

Turning off the main road and heading toward the lake, Bryce tried to shake off the guilt he always felt on thinking about it, but this time, he simply couldn't. If he had been with his mother that last night, she wouldn't have disappeared.

He'd ignored the soul-searing warning, the absolute knowledge that something was wrong, and he'd never been able to forgive himself.

Since then, Sheelin O'Keefe's prophecy had hung over his head, waiting for him to make another mistake. Sometimes he could feel it—whenever he was with a woman who seemed just a little too right for him. Like Hailey. Especially Hailey. The weight of their having sex the night before had ignited some internal mechanism, a warning that he was close to triggering the curse.

He felt more than a little something for

Hailey and he feared for her and he was going to have to let her go.

Now.

Before it was too late.

Before he fell in love with her.

Pulling into his drive, he parked and headed for the door off the kitchen, wishing Hailey were inside waiting for him. More and more, his thoughts centered on her. On what-ifs. What-ifs weren't possible. He wasn't going to put her in danger. He wasn't going to be responsible for something terrible happening again to someone he cared for.

No sooner did he step into the house than his phone rang.

Caller I.D. told him it was Croft.

"I'm going hunting up in your area and thought you could meet me there. And bring your lovely wife."

"Hailey's working." Truthfully, Bryce didn't think of killing an animal as sport. He never had, not even in the days when he'd gone along with his friends because it was expected of him. Not that he'd ever killed any creature himself. "And I haven't hunted in years."

"Well, it's time you got back to it." Croft

paused and when Bryce didn't agree, said, "I insist."

Bryce clenched his jaw. How had he gotten himself into this situation? The man was determined to run his life.

Trying to get out of it without severing the connection, he said, "The problem is that I no longer have a license."

"Not a problem at all. I'm headed for a private preserve on the state line. I assume you know Grainger Hunt Club."

"I know *where* it is." Twenty minutes or so south of the lake.

"Then I expect to see you there in an hour. You'll be my guest. And don't worry about not having your own equipment. I have several bows with me, so you can borrow one. Tell your lovely wife to join us when she's free."

He wanted Hailey to come? No doubt he meant to question her about Widow's Peak again. Not seeing how he could get out of this without offending Croft and ruining any chance of saving McKenna Development, Bryce caved.

"I'll see you there."

Croft's tone held a hint of glee when he said, "I thought you would."

HAILEY'S schedule for the afternoon was clear, so she thought to walk over to the police department. The day was gray, the air cooler than she liked. Dark clouds formed in the sky, but rain didn't look imminent, so she kept going on foot. She would see what information she could wheedle from the chief of police. Arnold Schmidt had worked for the department since he was a rookie. If anyone could tell her about Croft, it would be Schmidt.

Halfway there, she brought her plan to an abrupt halt when she spotted Iceman leaving a bar and heading in the opposite direction. Hailey power-walked after him, and just as the loan shark was about to cross the street, she caught up to him and grabbed his arm, spinning him around to face her.

"I have something to say to you."

The loan shark grinned at her. "Well, if it ain't Danny's very generous little sister."

"Stay away from my brother."

The grin faded. "I don't take no orders from no woman."

"Danny is trying to clean up his act, so you leave him alone!"

"Chill, baby."

But despite the attention she was getting

from passersby on the street, Hailey wasn't done. "Don't come up here again to invite Danny to another of your games. You won't get any more money from my husband or me, so sucking my brother back into some big game is not worth your while."

Iceman laughed. "You don't want nothing to happen to your brother, so I know you would find the money to rescue him again."

Furious, Hailey asked, "Remember the detective who came to see you in Chicago? Reilly McKenna is my brother-in-law and he would *love* to make your life miserable. Which he will if you let Danny into one of your games. And stay out of Lake Geneva. This is *my* town. These are *my* people. Don't come after Danny again or I'll make your life miserable here."

"Who says I came to Lake Geneva for a loser like your brother?" Iceman said, taking a threatening step closer.

Hailey's pulse jumped, but she stood her ground.

"I know people here, too," Iceman said. "Chicagoans who have summer homes on the lake. I've been collecting from their deep pockets for more than a dozen years and I'm not about to stay away because you say so."

He backed off. "Want to take my photo now? Got a cell phone that works?"

Why was he taunting her about her cell?

When she didn't answer, he crossed against the light, holding out his hand for vehicles to stop and let him pass. A frustrated Hailey stared after him, wondering about those contacts of his around the lake.

And he'd known about the cell phone… So had it been him? Had Iceman thrown her in the river?

To kill *her*…or her cell phone with those photos she'd taken of him?

Another question to ask Chief Schmidt— she wondered if he knew about illegal gambling in the area. She wondered if he knew about a loan shark coming up here, into his town. She marched over to the building housing the police department and asked to see him. Luckily, Schmidt had just returned from a late lunch and was available. He invited her into his office.

Sitting in his beat-up leather chair, his white mustache twitching above a smile, he asked, "Hailey, what can I do for you?"

"I'm trying to get some background on a potential client," she told him. "I didn't think he'd ever been to Lake Geneva before, but it seems his family used to rent a house on the lake."

Schmidt rocked back in his chair and gave her a piercing look. His faded blue eyes seemed to bore into her. "What exactly is it that you want to know?"

"The reason they stopped coming more than a decade ago." She sat in the chair on the other side of his desk. "The name is Croft. Apparently one of the sons got into some kind of trouble. I like to know who I'm dealing with."

"James Croft," Schmidt mused. "I remember him. He was only seventeen at the time. There'd been a series of break-ins around the lake all that summer. Anyway, Frank Bell caught the Croft kid and Mike Anderson inside his house when he came back into town in the middle of the night. He pulled a gun on them and brought them in."

So not only was James Croft a thief, but he also knew Mike Anderson and apparently very well. Not that he'd said so. And Mike had been a thief as well. Then something else struck her.

"The Bell mansion…that's the place next to Widow's Peak, right?"

"That it is."

She was getting a really weird feeling about the connection. "So what happened?"

"They hadn't actually stolen anything before getting caught, and the damage was minimal, so Frank Bell wouldn't press charges. They got a sound lecture and a pass, and the parents had to pay for the broken window. A few days later, Croft's parents got the family out of town and never came back. We couldn't prove anything about the other break-ins, but they stopped after the family left."

"So James Croft is a thief."

"He was a kid way back then. He was totally freaked out. Probably getting caught like that taught him a lesson."

But Hailey wondered if Croft had changed or if he'd stepped up his life of crime. She also wondered even more about his interest in Widow's Peak, considering one of the owners was his former partner in crime. Certain that Bryce wouldn't want to get involved with dirty money, she had to tell him about this.

"Come to think of it," Chief Schmidt said, "all that happened more than a dozen years ago. Fifteen to be exact."

"Wow, you have some memory."

"I remember because of what else happened that night."

Hailey's stomach tightened. "What else happened?"

"It was the same night Alice McKenna disappeared."

## Chapter Twelve

No sooner did she leave the chief's office than Hailey pulled out her cell phone to call Bryce. She saw there was a voice mail from him. Annoyed that the cell hadn't rung, she retrieved the message.

*"Hailey, Croft called and insisted I hunt with him today. He wants you to join us as well. If you can get away, meet us at the Grainger Hunt Club. I'm already on my way."*

They went hunting? Shuddering, she checked the time. Bryce had called only twenty minutes ago, while she was talking to Chief Schmidt. She returned the call but it went to voice mail.

"Bryce, I need to talk to you, but I'll be on my way to the Grainger Hunt Club as soon as I can get home and change out of my work clothes. Call me."

Turning to go, Hailey almost ran into Ray Anderson.

"What's going on?" Ray asked.

From the look on his face and his proximity to Schmidt's office, Hailey wondered if Ray hadn't overheard their conversation about the thefts and the reference to his brother.

She forced a smile. "Just keeping good relations with local law enforcement. What are you doing here?"

"Delivering a late lunch to some of the men."

Indeed the officers behind the front desk were just opening foam containers filled with burgers and fries.

"Hailey, about your brother…"

Uh-oh, what had Danny done now? Hailey tensed. "What about him?"

"He's interviewing with me on Friday."

"So he told me."

"The interview's just a formality. He's got the job. Just thought you'd like to know."

"Thanks, Ray." She almost hugged the man.

"I figured it was the least I could do. You know, with you working so hard for us before we even sign the contract on Widow's Peak.

I know Mike's been a pain in the butt about the whole thing."

"No problem. Hopefully I can have a proposal on the work to be done day after tomorrow."

"Why don't we go over to the estate now? You can point out the flaws."

"Sorry." She really was. She would like nothing more than to get this settled. Not that Ray had complete say. Backing toward the door, she said, "I have to meet Bryce and I'm late."

"Go ahead, then. You work on the proposal, and I'll work on Mike."

Hailey waved goodbye and left the building. She was home in less than ten minutes—Danny was gone—and out the door in another five. As she took a shortcut to the main road, she saw her brother's car parked in a drive next to a house in a secluded area.

What was Danny doing there?

Had Iceman set up a game that her brother hadn't been able to resist?

Realizing she'd forgotten to ask Chief Schmidt what he knew about the Chicago loan shark or about local illegal gambling, she decided she didn't have time to worry about him or Danny at the moment. That problem would have to wait.

On the drive south, the things she'd learned about Bryce's mother and about James Croft and about Mike Anderson whirled around and around in Hailey's mind until her brain was exhausted. How much of this could she tell Bryce? She remembered Grania telling her that Bryce for some reason continued to feel guilty about their mother's disappearance.

How could she tell him what she believed to be true about that night without it killing him?

Twenty minutes later, she checked in at the front desk of the Grainger Hunt Club. Several stuffed deer heads mounted around the room watched her from glass eyes, giving her the creeps.

"Ah, so you're Mr. Croft's other guest. He was anxious about whether you'd make it," the manager said.

She glanced at his nameplate, "How long ago did they start, Mr. Avery?"

Avery checked his watch. "Probably only ten minutes ago. Don't worry, if you hurry, you'll catch up to them." He opened a map and set it on the counter. "Mr. Croft said to send you this way." He pointed to the farthest western route and traced it with his finger. "He also said not to worry, he has extra equipment for you to use."

*As if!* Hailey shuddered at the idea of killing any animal. "Thanks," she said.

She took the map from him and was getting a better look when he picked up the phone and punched in a number.

A few seconds later, he said, "Mr. Croft, your guest is here. I'm sending her on the trail right now." Then to Hailey, he said, "He'll be watching for you."

"Good." She forced a smile that wouldn't convince anyone she was in a good mood.

Pulse fluttering, she left the clubhouse. The wind had picked up and dark clouds were now crowding the sky. Not the best weather for hunting or any sport. Her purpose was not to appease Croft and hunt with him, however, but to find Bryce, so that she could tell him what she'd learned about his would-be business partner. She'd have to get him alone or, even better, find an excuse so they could leave together.

If James Croft was capable of breaking and entering, what else might he be willing to do?

For all she knew, they were dealing with a sociopath.

Following the route the manager pointed out on the map, she circled the edge of a small lake where men in boats ignored the impending weather and wielded fishing poles in a leisurely manner. Her breath quickened as she entered a gray wooded area of red oak with an occasional hickory or black cherry tree. Her presence flushed brightly colored birds from the branches and she heard small animals scurrying close to the ground. Once she even saw the back end of a deer as it bucked and fled.

The forest was climbing uphill and so was she. The air was still, like nature was holding her breath. Hailey's own breath came in short gasps as she hurried, the harsh sound bouncing from tree to tree.

Why wasn't she hearing anything else? Like voices? Where were Bryce and Croft? She'd been moving so fast that she should have caught up to them by now.

To one side, she saw a clearing in the trees. She veered off toward the opening. Breaking from the forest, she noted an unobstructed expanse before and below her. She'd come out on a ridge that sloped down forty or fifty feet to a meadow below.

All was silent.

Wind whipped around her and sent a chill up her spine, and a frisson of fear skittered through her.

*Bryce...*

She pulled out her cell phone, but she couldn't scare up a signal. The call kept dropping. Even as she slipped the phone back into her pocket, the short hairs at the back of her neck stood on end and she froze.

Someone was watching her.

Hailey peered into the nearby forest, moving her gaze from tree to bush to tree, but she saw nothing, not even a squirrel. Although the quiet was deafening, Hailey was certain she wasn't alone. About to slip back into a stand of trees for protection, she heard the high, sharp *thwang* too late.

Even though she bolted to the side, she couldn't get out of the way of the blur coming for her fast enough.

Hot pain seared her arm. The impact sent her flying backward.

Her feet came out from under her and she hit the ground that sloped away from the ridge hard. Unable to stop herself, Hailey threw her arms up over her head for protection and rolled over and over, not stopping until she hit flat ground.

For a moment, she couldn't move. The breath was knocked out of her. Her arm was bleeding where an arrow had grazed it.

Someone had tried to kill her!

Again!

She had to get out of there, had to get to cover. Forcing herself to sit up, she bit back a cry when pain shot along her arm. She took a deep breath and was about to get to her feet when footsteps thundered down the slope toward her. Looking up, she saw James Croft, bow in hand, quiver of arrows with bloodred feathers slung across his chest. He was heading for her fast.

He'd known she was coming because the manager had called him.

He'd said he'd be watching for her.

So he could kill her? Why?

Panic made her ignore the pain, and she somehow got her feet under her just as Croft reached out to grab her arm.

Had he come to finish her off?

# Chapter Thirteen

"No! Don't touch me!" Hailey slapped at Croft's hand.

When he saw the red splotch on the arm of her sweater, Bryce's heart almost stopped but his legs sped up.

"Hailey, please!" Croft protested. "I'm just trying to help you."

His gut clenching, Bryce yelled, "Hailey, I'm coming!"

He raced down the incline as Hailey scrambled away from Croft.

"She's hysterical," Croft told him. "Apparently some careless hunter let go an arrow without being certain he was shooting at a deer. I'm simply trying to help her."

"You tried to kill me!"

"I did no such thing!" Croft protested. "I heard a noise and thought maybe a deer was foraging around. I came into the clearing to check it out and you were already rolling down the hill!" He looked around. "No sign of whoever did this."

Feeling sick inside, not knowing what to believe, Bryce reached down and pulled Hailey up into the shelter of his body. Taking care of her now was his chief concern.

He could have lost her...

No matter who had tried to shoot her, in the end, he was to blame. He checked her arm. It was still oozing blood, and the sleeve of her sweater was ruined, but the wound itself didn't look serious. Thankfully, she'd only been grazed by an arrow.

It could have been so much worse.

"Can you stand on your own?" he asked.

"Yes, of course." Hailey stared at Croft as if to make certain the man didn't try to come near her.

Bryce took off his shirt and tied a sleeve around her arm, then placed the bulk of the material over the wound. This was his fault. He never should have married her. Never should have given in to his physical needs the night before. Hailey was lucky she hadn't been hurt worse.

Or killed.

"Give it as much pressure as you can to

stop the bleeding." He hooked an arm across her and curled his fingers around her waist.

As if that could protect her.

"I can help," Croft said, stepping toward them.

Hailey flinched.

"Leave her be!"

Croft backed off and threw his hands up in the air. "All right, but I'm telling you I didn't shoot that arrow."

After that, Croft fell silent, but Hailey kept darting looks at him all the way back to the clubhouse, where Bryce filled out an accident report while an in-house medic took a look at her arm. Fortunately, it had stopped bleeding. The medic cleaned and bandaged the wound, which he declared was little more than a bad scrape. He said she needed a tetanus shot and an antibiotic as soon as possible, however, and gave them the name and address of a local clinic.

When they came out of the medic's room, Croft was nowhere in sight. Now where the hell had he gone? Bryce wondered as he handed the report to Herman Avery, the manager.

"Where's Croft?" Bryce asked.

"Mr. Croft took a call and said he had to leave. He asked me to tell you he was sorry."

"He targeted me purposely and you just let him leave?" Hailey sounded outraged.

"I'm sure that's not true!" Avery cut in. "Mr. Croft said he had nothing to do with the incident, and that you were simply hysterical."

Wanting to keep her calm, Bryce placed a hand in the small of her back. "And yet we'd like an official investigation." His protective instincts were fully aroused.

Despite his vehement protestations, Croft could have shot Hailey, but surely if he had, it really had been an accident. Although how an investigation could prove that, he didn't know.

"Yes, of course." The manager looked at the report. "Okay, I know where this is. I'll call the sheriff and see if someone can come out here this afternoon to take a look."

"How generous of you," Bryce said, not bothering to temper the sarcasm in his tone. "Someone will have to drive my wife's car back to our home."

"I'm sorry." The manager looked at him as if he were an alien. "We don't do that sort of thing."

"If you don't want a lawsuit on your hands, find someone who does."

The manager choked and then said, "Yes, of course."

Bryce wrote down directions to the house. "Hailey, give the man your keys."

Hailey did as he asked, and then said, "Let's get out of here."

Above her protests that she would be fine by morning, Bryce got her to the nearby clinic where a doctor checked and rebandaged her wound, then gave her a tetanus shot and a prescription for the antibiotic and another for painkillers, which Hailey said she didn't need. Nevertheless, Bryce stopped at a pharmacy in town and filled both prescriptions just in case she was in pain later.

Rain splashed the windshield, but Bryce knew that nature was holding back for the moment, that they were in for a big storm later that night. He turned the wipers on low.

He waited until they were halfway back to McKenna Ridge before asking Hailey, "Why is it you think Croft aimed for you on purpose?"

"I'm not sure, but maybe it has something to do with my ability to contact the spirits at Widow's Peak. Croft has asked me about it more than once. Maybe he has reason to *not* want me to hear what they have to say."

"What are you talking about?"

"I believe a woman died there, Bryce, and not of natural causes."

A frisson of discomfort skittered up his spine. "You think someone had a fatal accident?"

"Or she was murdered."

"Hailey…aren't you being a little…dramatic?" At least he hoped she was.

"I'm telling you what I felt. And saw."

"Wait a minute. I thought you didn't *see* ghosts."

"The other night was the exception," she said. "I saw her just for a few seconds. She was bleeding from her forehead, Bryce. It looked like someone had hit her in the forehead with some heavy object. The whole side of her face and neck were covered with blood."

Bryce's discomfort deepened, but he didn't want to further investigate the feeling, so he ignored it. "I don't ever remember hearing of a murder at Widow's Peak," he said, realizing he had the steering wheel in a death grip.

"Maybe the death was never reported."

"How could that be?"

"What if her body wasn't found there?"

"If she was dumped in the lake—"

"No. I mean, what if her body is still on the grounds somewhere?"

Hailey's voice was strained, making Bryce wonder what she wasn't saying. "You think whoever killed the woman buried her on the property?"

"It's possible."

The idea gnawed at him. As much as he wanted to dismiss it, he couldn't. "What did this woman look like?"

"I didn't get a good look at her face, not with all that blood. All I know for certain is that she had long dark hair and that she was dressed in fairly modern clothes, which leads me to think she died in the last twenty years."

Although he believed in Hailey's ability to sense spirits in a house, Bryce was having difficulty making the connection she had. "So what does this have to do with James Croft?"

"When he was a teenager, his family used to rent a lake house for the summer. There were several break-ins that year, and Croft and Mike Anderson were caught inside Frank Bell's home in the middle of the night. That property adjoins Widow's Peak," she reminded him. "What if they broke in there, too, and the woman saw them?"

He took his eyes off the road just for a second, long enough to see that she was absolutely serious. "You think they killed her to keep her quiet?"

"I don't *want* to think it…"

Bryce felt as if his mind was scrambled. He'd always thought Mike was a decent guy, and while he had his issues with Croft, he just couldn't imagine the man committing such a heinous crime. His mind went around and around with the possibility as he pulled in the drive and parked next to Hailey's car. Apparently, the manager of the hunt club had been able to find someone to return it after all.

"Bryce, I have something else to tell you."

"About Danny? I saw Ray earlier. He told me he's giving your brother a job."

"I know. It's not a great opportunity for the future, but it's a start. Now if only Iceman will stay away from him."

Bryce shrugged. "As long as Danny remains in Lake Geneva, that doesn't seem like a problem."

He got out of the car and walked around to her side, then, despite her protests, helped her out. When she almost stepped into him, his gut tightened and he had to fight from putting his arms around her.

Lightning lit her beautiful face for a few seconds. Thunder rumbled, the rough sound making him want to act. Rain droplets danced along her forehead and cheeks, but she didn't seem to mind. And the way she was looking at him, eyes wide, lips parted, made him want to take her in his arms...

*C'mon, Bryce, loosen up. I know you want to. I want it, too, so kiss me already.*

Hailey's thoughts set Bryce on fire. But after what had happened at the hunt club, he couldn't indulge himself again. Couldn't take any more chances with her life. Holding himself in tight control, he backed away from her.

She blinked and her hopeful expression closed.

Just then, Bryce's cell phone rang. Fetching it, he checked the caller I.D. "Mr. Avery, did the authorities come out to investigate?"

"They did, Mr. McKenna, and they found the arrow with your wife's blood."

"And?"

"And the feathers were blue and gold. Not Mr. Croft's color."

Bryce remembered Croft's arrows had red

feathers. His own had been green. "Anything else?"

"Nothing decisive. They found several sets of footprints in the area. A party of five was on that route this morning."

"Thank you, Mr. Avery. If anything else comes of it, please keep me informed."

"Very well, sir. I'm sure you'll be hearing from someone in the police department as well. We did return your wife's car as requested."

"So I see."

When the manager hung up, Bryce related the news to Hailey.

"So it wasn't Croft after all," she said. "Unless…he could have found someone else's arrow and used it."

"But that doesn't seem likely."

He didn't like Croft, wished he'd never had to court the man, but that didn't make him a potential killer.

Hailey ducked her head and swept by him and raced up the few steps to the walk while Bryce closed the passenger door and set the car alarm.

"Back to Iceman," she said. "Avery called before I could tell you that Iceman was here today."

Catching up to her, he asked, "In Lake Geneva?"

She nodded. "He tried to get Danny into a high-stakes game. Danny told him to get lost. *I* told him to get lost."

"What do you mean *you* did?" The drizzle turned to rain as he unlocked the door.

"I ran into Iceman on Main Street. I couldn't help myself. He said I wasn't going to stop him from coming to Lake Geneva and collecting from the deep pockets living around the lake. I don't remember seeing him before, but he said he's been coming here to see clients for years."

Hailey went inside and Bryce followed, trying to remember if he'd ever seen anyone who looked like Iceman in town. Not that he knew everyone who vacationed or visited here. Then again, maybe the loan shark didn't hang out in town but merely came to the lake houses to collect, then left once he had his money.

"When did all this happen?" he asked, following her into the family room.

"About a half hour before I left for the hunt club."

"Wait a minute." Bryce quickly put two and two together. "You had a public argument with him and an hour later someone aimed an arrow at your back."

"You don't really think it could have been Iceman?"

"Why not?"

"Where would he learn to use a bow and arrow?"

"Maybe he never did," Bryce said, walking to the windows and staring out at the lake. The storm had already kicked up. Rain deluged the area. "That would explain why a supposed hunter barely grazed you. That's twice now that you told Iceman off and then something happened to you right afterward. First you almost drowned and then you were almost shot. I'm going to call Reilly, see if he can't find a reason to get that man off the street."

"That's a good idea just in general. Even if he didn't try to hurt me, remember he threatened to kill Danny."

Thinking of *Hailey's* well-being, Bryce couldn't wait any longer. He couldn't wait until after she was killed. He turned to face her. "This is my fault, Hailey."

"What are you talking about?"

"Sheelin O'Keefe's curse on the McKennas. Since you got involved with me, you came close to being killed. Twice."

"But how could it be the family curse when you don't love me?"

Those words twisted his insides. He didn't know how he felt about her. Certainly not neutral. Certainly more than he had going into the marriage. But he *couldn't* love her. *Wouldn't.* Because if he did love Hailey, he would be condemning her, and he wanted to believe he could still let her go and she would be safe.

"How I feel doesn't matter, Hailey."

"Apparently it does."

Her wistful tone was like a punch to the gut. "Look," he said, "I vowed years ago never to fall in love."

"Because of your mother?"

"And because of the other McKennas who have lost the women and men they loved."

Too many to count. He'd heard the stories all his life, but he hadn't really believed until the prophecy had struck his own family. Losing his mother had changed him.

"Grania told me you feel guilty about your mom's disappearance," Hailey said, "but I don't understand. What did that have to do with you?"

"Nothing," he lied.

"I don't believe you. You can tell me, Bryce. You can tell me anything."

He'd never told another soul, not even Grania. But maybe it was time. Maybe he had to tell Hailey. Otherwise she would never believe him, would never let him do what he had to.

"I took a break from summer school, came home that weekend to go to a friend's birthday party. Mom asked me if I would go somewhere with her that night...not that she explained where she was going or what she was doing or why it was so important. She was being so mysterious, just saying there was something important she had to do— someone she had to see—and that she didn't want to go alone."

"But you wanted to go to the party."

He nodded. "That's why I came home. I wanted to be with all my friends. I asked her if we could do what she wanted the next day instead."

He'd done so despite the weird feeling he'd gotten inside—a warning, although he hadn't known it then.

"And she said yes," Hailey guessed.

"Of course. She told me it could wait, that I should go ahead and have a good time."

And he had.

His mistake.

If only he'd gone *with* her instead...

Hailey continued, "And then you never saw her again."

"No one ever saw her again. It was like Mom drove off into the rain and simply vanished. It was a night like this one," he said, turning back to the windows. The next strike of lightning lit the opposite shore and he got a brief glimpse of Widow's Peak. He walked away from the view, went to pour himself a drink. "It was Sheelin O'Keefe's prophecy come true, Hailey. Dad never got over it. And neither did I."

"I know how hard it is to lose someone you love. My mom's still alive, but she walked out of Danny's and my life. And our father walked out on us when we were just kids. They're still alive, but we lost them. I know I never got over that either."

"I can feel the curse inside me, Hailey. I felt it when my mother agreed to let me go to that party. Something told me not to...and I ignored it. I've felt it ever since.... I can't be responsible for another loss."

"What are you saying?"

"That I release you from our agreement. I'll start divorce proceedings tomorrow."

"Bryce, that's not necessary. It'll kill your deal with Croft."

"And if Croft is the one trying to hurt you? I brought him into your life!"

She took a big breath and shrugged. "What if he's not guilty? You're not to blame for anything. If Iceman came at me, that's on Danny. He put that in motion before our bargain."

"I can't take that chance. I want you to be safe, Hailey. You're not. I can feel it every time I'm around you. I won't lose you, too."

"Isn't that what you're doing by sending me away?"

"At least you'll be alive. You might feel the loss of your parents, Hailey, but they're not dead. You have the possibility of seeing them again someday."

"And will I have the possibility of seeing *you* again?"

Bryce clenched his jaw and didn't answer. Under other circumstances he would fight to keep her. But with her well-being…no, with her *life* in the balance, he would fight anyone to keep her safe.

Even Hailey herself.

For a moment, Hailey couldn't hide her stricken expression. Then she straightened up and put on her neutral mask. For a moment, he thought she was going to say something to extend the argument. But in the end she shook her head sadly and left the room to take refuge in her lower-level suite.

Then the whole truth hit him hard, and he had to fight himself not to go after her. Even though he'd been denying it to himself, he had fallen in love with his wife and had acted on it.

Her leaving wouldn't make a difference.

He'd already put her in mortal danger.

## Chapter Fourteen

Rejected again.

Hailey stood at the outside door to her suite and stared through the window into the rain. Her wounded arm aching, she took one of the prescription painkillers. She threw herself onto her bed and stared up at the ceiling for a long time. Her mind rolled over and over her situation.

How had this happened to her?

How could she have fallen in love with a man who'd married her as a business asset?

It wasn't like Bryce hadn't been honest from the beginning. He'd told her straight out that business was the only reason he would marry, that he considered her an asset. She'd thought she would be okay with that—anything to get her brother through one more crisis—but she simply wasn't okay. She'd let her feelings get the better of her, and the night before, in the wave pool, she'd thought Bryce had as well.

Then she'd realized how wrong she'd been. He hadn't felt anything for her, at least not in the way she'd hoped. She'd thought he'd simply been all about the money, but she was no longer convinced it was that simple. He wanted success, obviously, but now she wondered if it wasn't a matter of substituting his business for the family he'd vowed never to have. Considering the burden of guilt he'd taken on himself over his mother, she couldn't really fault him.

And now guilt was making him shove *her* out of his life. Finding those articles about his mother's disappearance in Violet's scrapbook had brought that guilt to the fore, and all it took was the incident at the hunt club to make him believe that he was responsible for her life as well. Perhaps she should be flattered or grateful that he cared enough to want her to be safe, but surely there was another way to do that and find some personal happiness.

Closing her eyes, she listened to the rain drum against the house. A sharp crack and a loud crash was followed by a threatening rumble. Lightning had struck nearby, probably felling a tree.

Was this the kind of storm that Alice McKenna had braved alone, despite her wanting her son to go with her? Had she driven to Widow's Peak to speak to Violet? Why? What had happened that fate-filled night?

Had James Croft broken into Widow's Peak only to be faced with a witness? Had he killed Alice? Alone?

Or had Mike Anderson helped him?

Where was Alice McKenna's final resting place?

The questions circled around and around in her mind until she thought she would lose it if she didn't get the answers. And there was only one way she knew how to get them. Like Alice before her, she wished for Bryce's company—or was it protection?—but knew she couldn't tell him what she was going to do or he would stop her.

She was on her own.

The bedside clock told her it was early yet—she could still hear Bryce pacing overhead. How soon would it be before he went up to his room?

How soon before she could leave the house without his knowing?

Fetching her cell phone, she tried Danny's number but he wasn't answering. The call went straight to voice mail. That worried her a bit, made her wonder if Iceman had gotten to him. Remembering seeing her brother at that out-of-the-way house that afternoon, she hoped she wasn't too late warning him.

"Danny, I had another close call today at the Grainger Hunt Club. I'm okay, just a flesh wound," she assured him. "The thing is, we think Iceman might have been responsible. For the river, too. Please be careful. Don't let him talk you into anything. Love you. Talk to you tomorrow."

She clicked Off, set her cell phone alarm, then closed her eyes and let herself drift…

Waking up after midnight, she listened intently. No sounds above. Hopefully Bryce was up in his suite on the second floor. She got up, washed her face, changed into a sweater that wasn't decorated with her blood and found a light slicker in the closet. The rain had stopped. For now.

Carefully, she opened the outside door and slipped out into the damp. It was as if the night were holding its breath. She held hers, too, as she climbed the hill to the driveway, checked to see that Bryce's bedroom light was off, then got into her car. Quickly starting it, she backed up far enough to turn it around and head out.

The road around the lake was still wet and slowed her down. It felt like it took forever to get to Widow's Peak, although the clock in the car told her it had been only twenty minutes. Her thoughts were of Bryce as she pulled in the empty drive and got out, flashlight in hand. Would she learn what had really happened to his mother all those years ago. And why?

The house stood dark and forbidding. Her pulse accelerated. Lightning cracked behind it over the lake, giving her the weirdest sensation that the house was rushing toward her.

The breath caught in her throat and she took a step back to regroup.

"It's only a house. No one home. Nothing to fear."

Steeling herself, Hailey headed for the front door, but one step on the porch and she froze in her tracks. What was it about this spot that made her blood run cold? Darkness enfolded her in its frightening grasp, and even though she wanted to move, to put the key in the door, something was holding her to the spot. Again. What was it?

She looked around the dark, half expecting

to see the woman who'd died here. Half expecting to see Alice McKenna. No ghosts tonight, at least not yet.

Trying again, she took a step toward the door when something pushed at her—invisible hands?—making her move to the left. The pressure didn't let up until she practically stood on the antique cast iron bootscraper. Sensing she was meant to take a closer look, she crouched down and reached out to pick it up by the figure of the dog on top. The moment her fingers touched the object, a horrible vision blossomed in her mind

*Alice McKenna screamed in terror and the heavy bootscraper crashed down on her forehead, silencing her forever.*

Hailey flew back against the porch rail and her heart thumped double time.

Staring at the innocent-looking antique, Hailey knew she'd just identified the murder weapon.

HAVING just fallen asleep, Bryce didn't want to awaken when the sound of an engine starting shattered the silence. He fought it as long as he could, tried to tell himself that he was merely dreaming when a vehicle pulling away from the house made him surface despite himself.

Bryce stumbled in the bathroom, relieved himself, then flushed his face with cool water, but he couldn't put the sound he'd heard out of his mind. Had he been dreaming or not?

Going to the window that overlooked the drive, he focused his bleary eyes. Only one vehicle sat outside the garage. His SUV.

Hailey's car was gone.

"What the hell?"

Bryce left the room and made his way down the stairs.

Had she actually packed up and left to go to her place in the middle of the night? And why not after he'd told her he was breaking their agreement, that he would file for divorce the very next day?

He hurried through the long kitchen and the hall, veering away from the family room to take the stairs down to Hailey's suite.

She, of course, was gone, but her things were still there. She hadn't packed to go home. She'd simply left. Maybe she'd send Danny to get her things in the morning.

Curiously defeated, Bryce climbed the stairs to the family room and crossed to the windows, stared out at the lake. How the hell was he supposed to go back to sleep now, with guilt nagging at him. He'd started this marriage-of-convenience business. He'd put Hailey in danger. Who could have predicted the situation that had thrown them together would have such lasting consequences. Such emotional baggage.

He'd been the one who'd said it was over, and yet he already missed Hailey.

He was damned if he let her go...*she* was damned if he didn't.

The torturous feeling had returned. A warning?

Just as he thought it, several strikes of lightning hit a single area on the other side of the lake and he hurt with the knowledge of where Hailey had gone and why.

Moving fast, he hurriedly retraced his steps back to his own bedroom, where he wasted no time in dressing.

He would have to get himself to Widow's Peak so that he could bring Hailey back before she got herself into more trouble. She had a head start, though, twenty minutes or more now. That meant she was already there.

He had to get to her and fast.

Which meant, rather than going out to the

drive for his SUV, he went out a lakeside door and hurried down the bluff to the dock.

The fastest way to get to Widow's Peak being straight across the lake.

ONCE inside the house, Hailey forced away the vision she'd had of the murder. She stood in the foyer for a moment, wondering if she should go back to the scrapbook or if there was anything else for her to learn there.

Compelled to go to Violet's room, she followed her instincts straight up the staircase. Before she even got to the door, the late owner's scent teased and surrounded her, and once more she felt as if she were being pushed to the desk, where she turned on a lamp and sat. Finally, she would finish what she'd started last Sunday. She would learn what Violet had wanted her to see when Mike had cut short her initial exploration of the house.

"Violet, I know you're here." Slowly she opened the middle drawer while tuning in to her surroundings. "What is it you wanted me to find?"

Compelled to search the drawer, she touched everything—a lace-edged handkerchief…an old-fashioned pen…an address book—but nothing spoke to her.

"C'mon, Violet, give me a clue here."

Something made her shove her hand all the way to the back of the drawer. Her fingers bumped something small and hard, and when she pulled it free, she thought she was looking at a pillbox. The moment she picked it up, she imagined a whispered *yes*.

Her heart raced as she stared at the box, enameled gold with a large violet-colored stone in the top. Was this the treasure that Mike had been seeking these last weeks. Had Violet somehow protected it from being discovered?

Opening the box, she stared at the contents. Not a pill but a tiny gold ring of a similar size and studded with a garnet chip. The second she picked up the ring, it came to her: the photograph of Alice McKenna in the article about her disappearance. Alice had been wearing a chain with four of these jewel-studded rings. This was proof that Alice had been here.

"So how did you get this, Violet? Did you find it after Alice was killed on your porch?" There was no longer any question in her mind as to the murdered woman's identity. "Did you know what happened to Alice?"

Sadness came at her in waves. Hailey

sensed Violet's spirit was right there, mourning with her.

Placing the jeweled ring back in the box, she snapped the lid closed and started to replace it where she'd found it in the drawer. But wait…the proof could disappear just like that, so se slipped the box into her pocket. When she got back to the house, she would give it to Bryce and tell him about the bootscraper. He would know how to handle things.

But before she left the house, she had one more area to check out.

The widow's walk.

Taking the flashlight from her pocket, Hailey went to investigate. At the top of the stairs, she discovered the rain had stopped. She swept her flashlight around, the beam cutting through fingers of fog that threatened to swallow the platform whole.

"What is it you want me to know, Violet?

She was drawn to the antique bench sheltered by the single wall. Nothing else to investigate up here.

"What am I looking for? Give me a clue."

She ran her hands along the face of the wood back, looking for some small hiding place. Instinct made her sweep lower. She checked the bench seat, but it was solid and didn't lift to reveal hidden storage. Crouching, she felt along the intricate carving. All solid. She ran her hands under the bench. Nothing there either.

"Unless you can be more specific, Violet, I give up."

Despite her threat, she didn't leave. She had to have missed something. Thinking about the age of the bench, she considered a secret compartment. More carefully this time, she fingered the carving an inch at a time. A piece just off center moved a hair. Concentrating, she was able to move it a bit more, enough to hear a click. Her heart thudded as a drawer popped open.

Hailey took a big breath and reached inside until her fingers touched something not wood. As lightning cracked overhead, she pulled out a book encased in a clear plastic bag. A light rain drummed along the rooftop and her heartbeat danced along with it.

Hearing the rush of her pulse in her ears, Hailey rose and sat on the bench where she pulled the book free and ran her flashlight beam over the worn leather cover. It opened easily to a page in the middle.

The book was handwritten, a journal of some sort. She checked the inside cover and found the name of the woman who had written it—Mary Ryan—and a dedication: To my daughters Violet and Alice…

BRYCE steered his boat through fog soup that thickened as he approached the southern shore of the lake. Drizzle added to his discomfort. His thoughts had been so concentrated on Hailey that he'd whipped out of the house without a poncho. At least it wasn't raining as hard as it had been earlier. Still, streaks of lightning punctuated by a rumble of thunder continued to follow him as he sped across the lake on his rescue mission.

Hopefully he'd find Hailey and get her out of there before the rain kicked up once more.

Hopefully she wouldn't fight him on this.

His gut was giving him a bad feeling, though, and he always trusted his gut. He didn't know where it was coming from or what it was, but he sensed danger, just as he had the night Hailey had been thrown in the river. Considering she'd been wounded that afternoon, he wasn't certain she had any fight left in her. Why she'd come out here alone, he couldn't fathom.

It wasn't that he didn't know the reason. Of course she wanted to commune with the spirits, find out what had happened to whom. He wanted to know the answers himself. What if his mother had been here the night she'd disappeared, and what if the Bell mansion wasn't the first that Croft and Mike had broken into that night? What if the unthinkable had happened at Widow's Peak and, as if killing an innocent woman hadn't mattered, the thieves had gone on to their next target?

Bryce was certain his mother had died at Widow's Peak, that her body was there on the property somewhere.

If only everything made more sense.

Like why would Hailey put herself in danger? he wondered again.

Maybe she couldn't help herself. Maybe she was simply in the throes of the McKenna curse and had no will to fight it.

If so—and if anything happened to her— he would never forgive himself.

The pressure inside him, the one that seared his soul, increased triple-fold, telling him that she was most certainly in danger now.

Suddenly realizing that, even though he couldn't really see it yet, he was getting close to the shoreline, Bryce slowed, then when he saw a vague outline too close for comfort, he cut the engine and let the boat drift in on its own. A minute later, a thunk and a jerk told him that he'd hit land somewhere near Widow's Peak. He didn't have time to mess around trying to find the dock, so he anchored the boat, grabbed the all-weather flashlight, got out in calf-deep water and sloshed to shore.

Certain the estate was somewhere to the right of where he'd landed, he set off in that direction. His flashlight wasn't doing a damn thing for him—the beam went nowhere in the fog, so he turned it off and was clipping it to his belt loop when he heard a voice.

*What the hell is she doing here?*

Bryce froze. She? Did the mystery man mean Hailey? Bryce hadn't recognized the voice.

*Damn it all, she's probably doing her mumbo jumbo...however it is she communicates with the spirits!*

So he was talking about Hailey, whoever he was. Croft? Mike? Iceman? Danny? Bryce still couldn't figure out who was speaking. Was the man talking to himself or was someone with him?

*The bitch is going to ruin everything! Not if I can help it. She needs to be taken care of. Tonight. Third time's the charm.*

Bryce realized he was hearing thoughts, the reason he didn't recognize the voice of the man who'd already tried to kill Hailey twice. His pulse picked up and his gut went tight. He had to stay calm and get to his wife as fast and as silently as he could.

Grateful that the fog was just starting to lift, he moved swiftly toward the bluff. He got impressions of tree silhouettes and a bulky outline of a nearby structure in the lake that must be the dock. What he couldn't see was the man. Or where he was walking, Bryce thought when his foot caught on a downed tree limb and he nearly went flying. Thankfully he caught himself without making more than a whisper of sound.

He congratulated himself halfway up the hill. Only then did he hear a twig crunch behind him. He whipped around to face the villain, only to have something hard whip into his head.

Making him see stars and a black maw coming for him…

## Chapter Fifteen

Violet and Alice sisters?

Hailey read the dedication again. How could this be? She'd asked Bryce if his mother and Violet had been good friends and he hadn't thought so. He certainly had no idea that they were related.

She turned back to the page in the middle where the journal had opened so naturally, as if someone—Violet?—had read and reread the pages dozens of times.

Even shining the flashlight on the missive, she strained to read the handwriting.

*I've kept my secret to myself for decades, but as I get closer to the end, the truth wears on me. I want to tell them all, but I worry I would destroy lives by doing so.*

*I was only fourteen when Violet was*

*born. In those days abortions weren't legal and girls had no means of keeping a baby on her own. Either the grandmother claimed the child as her own, or it was given up for adoption. My own mother was already dead, so I gave mine up. I wanted my daughter to have a good home, with two loving parents. I thought she would be adopted elsewhere, that I would never see her again.*

*But the Andersons were childless. They adopted her and named her Violet. Eight years later, Mrs. Anderson got pregnant and had a boy, so Violet had a little brother. Now, though Violet never had children herself, she has family in her nephews Ray and Mike.*

*And she has another family of which she knows nothing. My family. Ryans and McKennas. She has a much younger half sister, Alice, plus blood nephews and a niece...*

Hailey's breath caught as she realized the implication. Violet Anderson Scott had been Bryce's aunt. Her mind raced. Is that what had been so important that Alice had come here without him—to meet her sister? Had she just learned the truth because she'd finally read her mother's journal?

If so…

Then why had Alice been killed?

Only one thought occurred to her: The murderer hadn't wanted Violet to have another family.

That had to be it.

As to why she herself had been a target for the last week…everyone knew she could commune with dead people.

The murderer must have feared her involvement in selling the house. And perhaps the murderer had known there had been proof and had been searching for this journal—the real treasure—and feared that she might do so before him.

The rain came down in earnest now. Quickly slipping the journal back into the plastic bag, Hailey replaced it in the secret drawer and secured it. It would be safe there until Bryce could come out here with Chief Schmidt and resume the investigation of his mother's murder.

Surely Schmidt would figure out the identity of the murderer. Had Mike killed Alice

McKenna so the estate wouldn't be split, with half going to Bryce's family? Or had Croft been caught breaking into Widow's Peak and had killed Alice to keep her quiet?

Something about all that felt wrong, though. Croft had been with Mike. Why would they—or one of them—kill the woman who'd caught them breaking into the mansion and then simply go on to the next house to rob rather than getting out of Dodge?

But what other explanation was there?

If only they had Alice McKenna's body, perhaps there was some way of figuring out who'd actually killed her.

If only *she* could tell them where the body had been buried.

Filled with dread, Hailey returned to the first-floor parlor.

"Alice, I know you're here. I know you came to tell Violet she was your sister. And I know what happened to you. But knowing isn't proof. Your children need to be able to bury you. Bryce needs closure. Please, help me one more time. Lead me to your grave."

Instinct made her leave the parlor, but rather than going to the front door, she found herself being nudged down a hallway to the mud room. For a moment she stood there, wanting to go to the outside door but finding herself drawn to the basement instead. She opened the panel that hid the doorway and switched on the light. Her chest tightened as she stepped down into the dank, barely lit space.

The darkness did more than surround her. It entered her. Tied her insides in knots. She felt the same way she had on the steps and in the front parlor. No, worse.

Careful to avoid the spiderwebs, Hailey walked around the basement, searching every corner for something suspicious. Waiting for some kind of sign that this was it. This was Alice McKenna's resting place. Nothing. She wanted to leave. Wanted to get out of the house. Wanted to go back to McKenna Ridge and tell Bryce what she'd found.

She went back to the staircase fully intending to do all that.

She couldn't take the first step up.

Lightning off the lake lit her from the inside. Thunder rumbled around and through her. Feeling electrified, she circled the basement again, in the end stopping at the two doors she'd noted before. She wanted to use the one that would take her to the outside where she could breathe and feel fully alive.

Instead Hailey opened the other one—the door to the coal bin.

Reaching inside along the door frame, she found a switch. A single, low-watt bulb lit. She didn't know what she'd expected to find, but it hadn't been this—more than half the eight-by-twelve room was filled with coal that had been dumped from the window above. Coal that must have been there since well before she'd been born.

Almost relieved, Hailey tried to step back but felt as if she were fighting an invisible force keeping her there, nudging her in the opposite direction. For a moment, darkness threatened to overwhelm her. She felt sick inside. Nauseous. Shaky.

Fighting back her fear, Hailey found a shovel and stepped to the edge of the coal pile.

She knew what she had to do.

She started digging.

Blindly.

With everything she had left in her, she tossed shovelfuls of coal to the side. She ignored the ache in her arm kicked up by the effort. Black dust billowed around her, threatening to choke her, but she didn't stop. She shoveled like her life depended on it. And still, when the defining moment came, when as much coal was piled to the side as was in front of her, and the first glimpse of white shone dully through the black shards, she experienced a moment of shock.

Hailey set the shovel against the inner wall containing the coal and began digging with her bare hands, raising more dust until she uncovered bone—fingers and then a hand, and then an arm. She threaded her fingers around what had once been a flesh-and-blood hand.

"Alice, I'm so sorry. But I found you now and Bryce and his family will finally know what happened to you. They can give you a proper burial, and I hope you can find some rest at last."

A sound behind her told Hailey she wasn't alone. She froze.

"I was afraid this was going to happen, so I decided to check on the house, figuring you wouldn't be able to stay away from the ghosts."

"Ray."

Pulse racing, she got to her feet and faced the man who she now knew had murdered Bryce's mother. The man who'd tried to kill her twice now. He was close enough to hit her over the head as he had Alice McKenna. And he undoubtedly meant to do just that.

"Why, Ray? Why did you kill Alice?"

"I overheard the McKenna woman making overtures to Aunt Violet about being family and all. Violet didn't need anyone but us, and I had plans for this place. I didn't need any more relatives claiming what was mine."

"Yours? You mean yours and Mike's. Does he know?"

"Are you kidding? Mike's clueless. He thought finding old crap in the house was a big deal. He had his period as a petty thief— him and Croft. Croft saw me murder Alice, although he didn't know it was me. He confided in me after he and Mike were arrested. I convinced Croft not to tell the police anything or they might think he and Mike were killers and not just thieves. Surprised the hell out of me when he came back and wanted to buy the place. Guilty conscience." Ray laughed.

So Ray had acted alone. Wondering how she was going to get out of this situation alive, Hailey tried to keep him talking to stall him until she could figure out how to get past him, how to get away. "But if Violet had a will—"

"Wills can be changed!" he cut in, leaning closer. "And challenged by high-priced lawyers. Alice McKenna was blood to Aunt Violet, but we weren't, because she was adopted into the Anderson family."

"That wouldn't have mattered to the courts," Hailey choked out. Too bad that, this time, Bryce wasn't around to hear her frantic thoughts. "And that's assuming the McKennas even cared about some inheritance."

"I couldn't take a chance on the courts. And everyone cares about money."

"Some more than others."

Behind him, the black dust above the coal she'd tossed to the side reminded her of the dust motes in the parlor. Hailey gasped. The dust was moving, forming into a familiar shape. Giving her hope that there was still a way out of this mess.

"Behind you," she whispered. "Alice…"

"Ah, don't give me any bull." But Ray's expression looked more fearful than disbelieving. "You don't think I'm going to fall for that?"

"Isn't that why I was so dangerous to you?" She glared at him. "The reason you tried to get rid of me? Because you knew I could communicate with the dead?" She turned her gaze back to the coal pile beyond him.

Hailey's eyes widened as an image took

form. A woman with long, dark hair hiding one side of her face, blood covering the other—the same woman she'd seen the other night.

"Alice?" Desperate to get Ray off balance, she asked, "What are you going to do to him?"

Expression grim, Ray couldn't help himself. He turned to look, then gasped and teetered on his feet.

Hailey grabbed the shovel, gripped the wooden handle like a baseball bat, aimed and swung it as hard as she could. She landed the metal square between Ray's shoulder blades. With a yelled oath, he flew forward, his body shattering the fragile image of Alice. He landed in the pile of coal, dust choking him.

Hailey ran out of the bin to the other door, the one that would take her outside.

Coughing, Ray yelled, "You'll pay for that, bitch!"

Her fingers fumbled on the locks. She could hear Ray struggling with the chunks of coal tripping him as he tried to get back to his feet. Hopefully seeing Alice threw him off his game. Finally the lock cooperated and Hailey tugged open the door and ran out into the rain.

"I'll find you!" Ray promised. "There's nowhere you can hide from me!"

He'd expect her to go back uphill to her car, so she went the opposite way, to the water. *The boat!* she thought, knowing there was always a boat anchored at the dock. *I'll grab the boat!* And hopefully, she'd be able to find the keys.

She ran, stumbled, slid downhill feet first, then landed on her hip and continued to slide. By the time she got halfway down, she was covered in mud.

Lightning fingered the lake. Hailey cursed and threw a glance over her shoulder. Sure enough, Ray broke free of the house just then and spotted her straight off.

Back on her feet, Hailey was going downhill so fast that she feared she would trip again.

And then she would be done for.

GROANING, Bryce came to with a hell of a headache and imagining that he heard Hailey's voice. And that he was drowning.

He whipped his head up out of a puddle and took a choked breath.

How long had he been out?

He was soaked to the skin and was starting

to shiver. Thankfully the rain had let up, leaving fingers of fog rising from the ground.

He struggled to his feet, his head feeling like it had doubled in size. He slid a hand to the back of his neck and slid it up carefully until he found a lump that was tender to the touch. His head went light and woozy.

It suddenly came back to him that he'd been in pursuit of Hailey.

Where was she?

Light glowed from several windows of the Widow's Peak mansion. He stumbled forward. He needed to get to his wife, to save her from the curse. The wet ground squished beneath his feet.

Was Hailey alone or had the bastard who'd clocked him already found her?

"Talk to me, Hailey," he muttered, concentrating on her as he ran faster toward the house. "C'mon, I need to hear that you're all right."

*Please, please, please, let me get to Bryce before he can catch up to me! Let me find the damn keys to the boat!*

Startled at the instant response, Bryce nearly tripped over his own feet and barely caught his balance as he slid to a halt.

Boat…

The lake!

He changed directions and headed for the shoreline even as he heard an engine crank and speed up. Lightning flickered over the lake, and for a second, he saw Hailey a dozen yards out, heading her craft toward the north shore.

And at the dock, Ray Anderson was getting into a second boat and hauling anchor.

Wanting in the worst way to call out to warn Hailey, Bryce forced himself to remain silent and adjust his course yet again. His own speedboat was a hundred yards in the opposite direction. He moved fast. Not fast enough. He heard the second engine kick in and knew Ray was after Hailey.

Seconds later, he threw himself into his boat, started his engine and yanked up the anchor. Then he was off across the foggy lake, guided by instinct and the occasional flicker of lightning.

His speedboat and engine were lighter and therefore faster than most on Geneva Lake. Halfway across, he got within shouting distance of Ray and was gaining rapidly.

The bastard had a heavy comfort boat and couldn't overtake Hailey, but he'd brought a gun, which he was now pointing at her back.

Ray was undoubtedly waiting for a lightning strike to give him enough light to improve his aim.

His stomach clenching, Bryce knew there was only one thing he could do stop Ray and to stop the curse from taking the woman he loved.

He stomped on the accelerator, feeling the boat lift a hair above the water. He hydroplaned it in a big arc.

Shouting, "Ray!" to get the man's attention off Hailey, Bryce took aim.

He got Ray's immediate attention. The bastard swung his gun arm around and aimed it at Bryce. He shot over and over, missing his target, but nicking the windshield more than once.

"Bryce!" Hailey yelled.

Bryce said a fast prayer before plowing straight into the middle of Ray's boat.

Hailey's horrified scream was the last sound he heard…

## Chapter Sixteen

"Bryce!"

Hailey frantically circled to where the other two boats collided and broke apart, raining metal everywhere. Flames shot up from the wreckage, and she steeled herself for the explosion that didn't come.

"Bryce!" she yelled again as she cut her engine, quickly turned on all her boat lights and aimed her flashlight beam everywhere. No sign of either man.

If she were to try to save Ray, would he hold her under the water until she gasped her last breath?

Unable to pierce the fog to know if there was another boat on the lake, she laid on her horn. When there was no answering blast, she dived in blindly toward the wreck site. She estimated nearly two minutes had passed.

If Bryce had been underwater all that

time…he only had somewhere between three and five minutes before he drowned.

Surfacing mere feet from a ripped-apart hull, she yelled, "Bryce!" and then went down again, going deeper this time, reaching out with both hands in every direction. No matter how deep she went, no matter how close she got to the wreckage, no matter how many times she tried, she came up empty.

An eerie sensation suddenly floated through her, twisting her chest into what she thought of as a big knot of grief. The weird feeling intensified, sadness gripping her from the inside out. She'd felt this way on entering Widow's Peak. Finally understanding came to her.

"No, Bryce, no!" she cried.

A sob caught in her throat as his spirit washed over her and through her, and she sensed that he was at peace with what he'd done.

He'd given his life to save hers.

"Let me find you, Bryce, please let me find you!"

She could bring him back—she knew she could—but she didn't have much time.

Taking a deep breath, she opened her mind to him and went under to seek his spirit and, hopefully, his body as well. She moved by instinct, knowing that when the grief shadowing her increased to an almost-unbearable degree, she was close enough to reach out and touch him.

Her hand brushed something smooth. She lunged closer. Bryce's face. Caught under the hull, his body hung there, and when she grabbed him and slung her arm over his chest to pull him to the surface, she felt no heartbeat.

Wanting to scream her grief, she held it in. She had to conserve her energy, had to pull him up out of the water into the boat. It wasn't too late, *couldn't* be too late. She would bring him back. She would!

They broke surface together, Hailey gasping, Bryce deadly silent.

A horn blasted at her and she realized a boat was coming straight for them. Then hands were reaching down and she was blindly pushing Bryce's body up, ignoring the pain it caused her wounded arm.

"Hailey, are you all right?"

"Danny!"

Her brother reached down for her and pulled her out of the water. He helped her lay Bryce on his back on the floor of the boat so they could work on him.

As Hailey positioned herself to administer CPR, Danny said, "I called the rescue team on my cell. What happened?"

Then it hit her. "Danny, Ray is still in the water!"

Her brother immediately jumped overboard.

"Be careful he doesn't try to hurt you!" she yelled, though she hoped under the circumstances, Danny could take care of himself.

Hailey gave Bryce two breaths, then compressed his chest for thirty seconds. She alternated breaths and chest compressions over and over, keeping the blood circulating until his heart could start pumping on its own. A light cut through the fog and a male voice hailed her. Even though she recognized it as belonging to one of the men on the lake rescue team, she didn't stop until Bryce gasped and began to breathe on his own. His heart pumped weakly beneath her hands.

Bryce's eyes fluttered open for a second. "Hailey, it's gone," he whispered, before his eyes closed again.

"What's gone?" she asked as a rescuer

jumped on board and took over for her. He checked Bryce's vital signs.

"He's lucky you got to him in time. Let's get him to a doctor." Signaling the rescue boat, he moved to take the driver's seat.

Hailey gasped, "Wait a minute—Danny."

"Where?"

"Here!" Danny yelled from the water. "I need a hand." Once they helped him topside, her brother said, "Sorry, sis, couldn't find Ray. It's impossible down there."

Hailey was sorry, too. Ray deserved to pay for what he'd done. Then again, she guessed he had with his life.

Sliding down next to Bryce, still unconscious—battered, bruised and bleeding but alive—she took his hand and kept track of his pulse in case his heart stopped again. "We'll start a recovery operation at first light. Get us out of here."

As the boat sped to the main town dock, Danny said, "I was worried when I heard your message, so I came to see you, but you were both gone. Then I heard that horn blast and went for the other boat."

"When you didn't pick up, I thought the worst," Hailey admitted. "That maybe Iceman got to you after all."

"I told you I wouldn't gamble again. I messed up, Hailey, big time. I can't believe I nearly bankrupted you. But I realized you and Bryce were right. I finally got professional help. I started seeing someone this afternoon."

That afternoon...when she'd spotted his car parked off-road and had assumed he'd gotten himself in another game.

"But enough about me," Danny said. "What the hell happened out there anyway?"

"Ray was going to kill me because of what I learned about Violet and Alice McKenna. They were sisters." Something that Bryce still didn't know. "Ray didn't want it known that his aunt had other relatives who could lay claim to the inheritance. I guess Bryce stopped Ray the only way he could."

Bryce had sacrificed his life to save hers.

Thank God she'd been able to bring him back.

Bryce woke up confused and hurting all over. The room was dark, but a window revealed the storm had passed and the sky was clearing. Moonlight filtered into the room, revealing a woman asleep in the chair next to his bed.

What the hell? Why was he in a hospital

bed, connected to an I.V., and why was Hailey keeping vigil?

It took him a moment to remember what had happened.

Hailey had almost died because of him. Because of the McKenna curse.

*The curse...*

Bryce remembered more. Remembered awakening in the boat to a startling discovery. "It's gone. It's really gone."

"What's gone?"

He reached out and grasped Hailey's hand and tugged. "Can you come closer for a minute?"

"Sure."

She got up from the chair and sat at the edge of his bed. He could see that her eyes were glassy, like she was trying not to cry.

"Closer."

She leaned in to him.

He hooked a hand around the back of her neck and pulled her close enough to kiss her. Their lips touching made him think of everything good that could happen between them now. When he let her go, he was grinning, at least as much as his bruised face would allow.

"The curse. I used to be able to feel it, especially around you. Not anymore."

Hailey stared at him a moment, swallowed hard and said, "You died in the water."

"I know. No white lights. Nothing so dramatic. But I swear I felt Mom. I swear she told me it wasn't my time and pushed me away, told me to come back."

"Thank God I found you when I did. Ray wasn't so lucky."

While he regretted the man's death, Bryce knew that if he hadn't stopped Ray, the man would have shot Hailey. "He killed my mother, didn't he? And he tried to kill *you* because he worried that her spirit would confide in you."

"You know it was Ray?"

"I didn't know for sure until I saw him, but when I went looking for you, I kept going over everything we'd learned and I just didn't believe the men we suspected were actually guilty. Then when I saw Ray go after you, it mostly fell into place. What I don't know is why."

"Your mom found this journal that belonged to her mother," Hailey said. "Alice learned that her mother had another child when she was very young. She gave her up for adoption."

"Violet?"

Hailey nodded. "Your mother's much older half sister. Ray overheard them talking about it and didn't want the McKennas messing up his plans for the money he and Mike were going to get when they inherited Widow's Peak."

"Greedy bastard! What about Mike?"

"Ray said he didn't know, that he acted alone." Hailey took something out of her pocket. "I'm actually amazed this didn't end up at the bottom of Geneva Lake."

She handed him what looked like a pillbox, saying, "I found this in a desk drawer in Violet's room. I think Violet found it after your mother was killed. Open it."

Bryce did so. His heart lurched when he recognized the contents.

"This is from the necklace we kids gave Mom for Mother's Day. There were four wheels, one for each of us with our birthstones. This one was mine." Staring at it for a moment, he remembered their giving her the present as if it was only yesterday. He touched it with a fingertip and swallowed hard. "Thank you for this. It means a lot to me. I don't want to lose it." He closed the box. "Will you keep it for me until I'm out of here?"

"No problem," she said, replacing the box in her pocket.

"What about the police?" he asked.

"While you were still in the E.R., I called Chief Schmidt and told him everything that happened with Ray…and where to find your Mom's body."

"I missed that part. Where, I mean."

"The old coal bin," she said. "Ray buried her under a ton of coal."

Bryce swallowed hard and figured that if she could see his eyes, she would know that he was now holding back tears. "We were that close to her body in the basement, and I didn't have a clue."

"Stop beating yourself up. You don't have to feel guilty anymore."

"How so?"

"Even if you had gone with her that night, Ray would have learned about the blood connection. His killing your mother wasn't a crime of passion. It was deliberate. If he hadn't done it that night, he would have found another time and place. Like he almost did with me. There was nothing you could do to stop it."

"Okay, no more guilt," he promised, his

eyes getting heavy. "Leave the rest till I get out of this place."

Hailey squeezed his hand and stayed put. Bryce took comfort in that as he let sleep take him.

A houseful of McKennas was challenging to say the least, but Hailey was glad Grania and Reilly and their father, Murtagh, came to gather around Bryce when he was to be released from the hospital. Only Liam, in the midst of investigating a kidnapping in New Orleans, was absent. If anyone had thoughts about why Bryce's wife didn't share his bedroom, they kept it to themselves.

Ray's body had been found. And what was left of Alice. They would finally be able to bury her in a few days.

Chief Schmidt had led an investigation as to what had happened on the lake. The bullet-scarred remains of Bryce's boat and recovery of Ray's gun had satisfied both him and the district attorney that there was nothing to prosecute. The case was already closed.

And Hailey had brought home Bryce's grandmother's journal.

Hailey had told his family everything she knew about Violet and Alice and the murder, but she kept some information to herself until Bryce returned home and they shared a buffet breakfast in the family room.

"I can't believe I lost my Alice out of that bastard's greed," Murtagh said, stabbing a sausage with his fork.

Looking at him, Hailey got a glimpse of Bryce's future looks—silver hair and eyebrows, but still handsome and distinguished, with smile lines at the corners of his eyes.

Grania gave her older brother a piercing stare. "People will do unconscionable things for money."

Obviously a jab at their marriage of convenience.

Hailey took a bite of her quiche and kept her thoughts to herself.

Murtagh cleared his throat, but his voice still sounded thick when he said, "What I don't understand is why my Alice never told me about Violet being her sister."

"Maybe she didn't know until right before the end," Hailey said. "And maybe she wanted Violet's permission to tell people first. I was thinking about why Alice might not have found the diary after her mother died," she said. "Then I figured it must have been in storage. I got a look at the basement here while doing laundry."

"And?" Bryce asked.

"I discovered an old hope chest. It looked promising, so I dug through it and found all kinds of interesting things including these."

She placed legal-size papers on the coffee table.

Closest to them, Grania took a look. "These prove Violet was given up for adoption, that she was Mom's older sister."

"And it proves this family has a stake in Widow's Peak," Hailey said.

"Violet left it to her nephews."

"Ray couldn't benefit from a crime," Reilly said.

Bryce countered, "But he didn't kill Violet."

"A lawyer would argue that Violet would have changed her will if Mom had lived," Reilly said.

"I took Mike's brother from him." Bryce's expression was grim. "I won't take anything else."

"You don't have to take anything, Bryce," Hailey said. She hadn't told anyone this yet—she'd wanted to wait until they were all together. "Mike is horrified at what his brother did. He came to the house yesterday to apologize. He hadn't had a clue as to what Ray was doing, but he feels he should have, that on some level he'd known things weren't right but he'd ignored the feeling. He offered to share the proceeds from the sale of Widow's Peak with Alice's children. Equal shares. He said it's the only way he can live with himself."

"Bryce, this would mean we don't need James Croft," Grania said. "Our shares of the money would put McKenna Development back on solid footing. We won't have to declare bankruptcy after all!"

"That's why you were courting Croft?" Hailey asked, amazed that he'd come up with the money to rescue Danny under those circumstances. "Because the company was going to go under?"

"Afraid so. I guess using what would have been Mom's inheritance is something we need to consider."

Hailey heard the hesitation in his voice. Easy money, but Bryce was torn about taking it. A fact that made her very happy. She had underestimated him, but she would never do that again.

They finished brunch and Murtagh and Reilly volunteered to be kitchen detail. They started by clearing the dirty dishes. Even though her arm didn't hurt anymore, Hailey let them do the heavy work.

"You look like you could use some more sleep," Grania told her brother.

"Actually, I could use some fresh air." Bryce gave his sister a penetrating look. "With my wife."

*Wife*...Hailey smiled.

Grania's eyebrows shot up. "Oh. Don't do anything foolish now."

He didn't ask her what she meant by that, just nudged Hailey toward the door. She was glad to leave the house and let Bryce lead her to the walkway. Hand in hand, they started down the bluff. She couldn't help but look across the lake to Widow's Peak. Since Alice's remains had been moved, the place had a whole different vibe for her. No more darkness. No more fear. The spirits were at peace, at last.

Halfway down to the water, Bryce said, "We need to talk."

"Uh-oh, that doesn't sound good."

"But it needs to be done, Hailey."

He stopped and cupped her shoulders with both hands and, wanting more, she swayed toward him.

"Maybe you could kiss me hello first."

Ignoring the suggestion, Bryce let his hands drop. "I want you to know nothing has changed. My offer to let you go stands."

"Wait a minute. You *still* want a divorce?"

"I'm willing to let you have a divorce per our agreement."

"Forget the agreement! I don't see our relationship as business anymore. What happened between us is very personal to me, and I don't want a divorce."

"Hailey…" Bryce's expression turned hopeful. "You're certain?"

Hailey stepped closer and wound her arms around his neck. "I love you, Bryce McKenna, and I probably always have at least a little since you stood up for me against those bullies when I was just a silly teenager. I'm not going to go unless you shove me out of your life. If you want to divorce me because you don't love me, that's on you. It'll be your decision, not mine."

"I *do* love you, Hailey. I'm crazy for you. I want to spend my life with you, have kids with you."

Exactly what Hailey wanted to hear. "Deal," she said, grinning.

"Deal."

Taking her in his arms, he kissed her—a deep, soul-stirring kiss—then nuzzled her ear and whispered in it.

"The curse killed me, but love brought me back."

\* \* \* \* \*

# LARGER-PRINT BOOKS!
## GET 2 FREE LARGER-PRINT NOVELS PLUS
## 2 FREE GIFTS!

### ◆Harlequin®

# INTRIGUE®

## BREATHTAKING ROMANTIC SUSPENSE

---

**YES!** Please send me 2 FREE LARGER-PRINT Harlequin Intrigue® novels and my 2 FREE gifts (gifts are worth about $10). After receiving them, if I don't wish to receive any more books, I can return the shipping statement marked "cancel." If I don't cancel, I will receive 6 brand-new novels every month and be billed just $5.24 per book in the U.S. or $5.99 per book in Canada. That's a saving of at least 13% off the cover price! It's quite a bargain! Shipping and handling is just 50¢ per book in the U.S. and 75¢ per book in Canada.* I understand that accepting the 2 free books and gifts places me under no obligation to buy anything. I can always return a shipment and cancel at any time. Even if I never buy another book, the two free books and gifts are mine to keep forever.

199/399 HDN FERE

| | | |
|---|---|---|
| Name | (PLEASE PRINT) | |
| Address | | Apt. # |
| City | State/Prov. | Zip/Postal Code |

Signature (if under 18, a parent or guardian must sign)

### Mail to the **Reader Service:**
**IN U.S.A.:** P.O. Box 1867, Buffalo, NY 14240-1867
**IN CANADA:** P.O. Box 609, Fort Erie, Ontario L2A 5X3

Not valid for current subscribers to Harlequin Intrigue Larger-Print books.

**Are you a subscriber to Harlequin Intrigue books
and want to receive the larger-print edition?
Call 1-800-873-8635 today or visit www.ReaderService.com.**

\* Terms and prices subject to change without notice. Prices do not include applicable taxes. Sales tax applicable in N.Y. Canadian residents will be charged applicable taxes. Offer not valid in Quebec. This offer is limited to one order per household. All orders subject to credit approval. Credit or debit balances in a customer's account(s) may be offset by any other outstanding balance owed by or to the customer. Please allow 4 to 6 weeks for delivery. Offer available while quantities last.

**Your Privacy**—The Reader Service is committed to protecting your privacy. Our Privacy Policy is available online at www.ReaderService.com or upon request from the Reader Service.

We make a portion of our mailing list available to reputable third parties that offer products we believe may interest you. If you prefer that we not exchange your name with third parties, or if you wish to clarify or modify your communication preferences, please visit us at www.ReaderService.com/consumerschoice or write to us at Reader Service Preference Service, P.O. Box 9062, Buffalo, NY 14269. Include your complete name and address.

HILPI1B

The series you love are now available in

# LARGER PRINT!

The books are complete and unabridged—
printed in a larger type size to make it
easier on your eyes.

◆ **Harlequin**® *Romance*

*From the Heart, For the Heart*

◆ **Harlequin**®
# INTRIGUE
**BREATHTAKING ROMANTIC SUSPENSE**

◆ **Harlequin**® *Presents*~

*Seduction and Passion Guaranteed!*

◆ **Harlequin**® *Super Romance*

*Exciting, emotional, unexpected!*

Try **LARGER PRINT** today!

Visit: www.ReaderService.com
Call: 1-800-873-8635

◆ **Harlequin**®

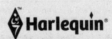 A *Romance* FOR EVERY MOOD™

www.ReaderService.com

HLPDIR11

# *ReaderService*.com

## You can now manage your account online!

- Review your order history
- Manage your payments
- Update your address

*We've redesigned
the Reader Service website
just for you.*

## Now you can:

- Read excerpts
- Respond to mailings and special monthly offers
- Learn about new series available to you

*Visit us today:*

# www.ReaderService.com

RS10